THE PORTRAIT

IAIN PEARS

HarperCollins*Publishers*

HarperCollins*Publishers*
77–85 Fulham Palace Road, London W6 8JB

www.harpercollins.co.uk

Published by HarperCollins*Publishers* 2005
1

First published in the USA by Riverhead
an imprint of Penguin Group (USA) 2005

A catalogue record for this book
is available from the British Library

ISBN 0 00 720276 8

Set in Dante

Printed and bound in Great Britain by
Clays Limited, St Ives plc

To Alex

Well, well, well. Come in, my dear fellow. Let me look at you. But first, an embrace; it is not often you see an old friend for the first time in nearly four years. You've not changed a bit. Well, of *course* I'm lying. The eyes are that little bit more lined, the skin has lost some of its texture, the hair is a touch more grey. We are both past our best. But at least you're still slim, to the point of emaciation. How you can eat so much to so little effect never ceases to astonish. The differences between us grow year by year, as you undoubtedly noticed the moment you saw me.

I must confess I was disturbed when I received your proposal last month. I thought, to begin with, that it was a bad idea. I could hardly believe you were prepared to travel all this way just to see me. Hence my cautious reply, in case you were making sly fun of me. My years of exile have made me sensitive, as you will no doubt discover. But here you are, a figure from history itself—my history, at least, as I suppose you are still very much in the centre of things back in London.

A glass of wine to toast your arrival. The pick of the Luberon. A particularly good year, 1912, as I am sure you will agree, especially when carefully aged for nearly nine months. I joke, of course. I like the stuff, but hardly expect your sophisticated palate to be equally enthusiastic. It is all sun and earth; no artifice in its production whatsoever. Dark, strong and somewhat violent—a little like the people who make it, in fact. I've grown used to the taste; it makes a change from the beer and cider that are the staples hereabouts, and fine vintages would be wasted on me, even if you could get them. I have a barrel brought over on the boat every month or so and drink it until it turns to vinegar. Already has, you think? No; it's meant to be like that—or if it isn't, few on this island know any better. This is the wine of the peasantry, the fuel of France. Drink it and you become like them. Don't say you haven't been warned.

Sit down, then. I know, not comfortable, but it is the cleanest and best chair I have. Besides, it will suit my purpose admirably, as you will see. I have been made nervous, even irritated, by your sudden arrival on my little island. Do you know how long it is since I've had a commission to paint a portrait? Extraordinary, considering my vogue, but I gave all that up when I gave up England. And now you want to take me into my past. So be it; you will have to endure the consequences of your own folly.

Your timing is as good as ever, though. A few months ago I would have rejected the idea out of hand, but now I found the invitation tickling. Why not, I thought? Let's see what we can do here. It is time to discover whether I can ever go back to England by exploring why I left in the first place. And who better to help the enquiry than the man who is the foremost critic in the land, whose opinion has the weight of the divine behind it?

Another little joke. But it is an opportunity to renew the battle and fight it to a conclusion. Who will emerge triumphant from this encounter of ours, do you think? The painter or the sitter? Will it be "portrait of a gentleman by Henry Morris MacAlpine," or "portrait of William Nasmyth, by anon." The National Gallery, or the National Portrait Gallery? We shall see. It will be your fame against my abilities, and the result won't be in until long after we're both dead. I won't trick you, I promise. I won't sign the picture and forget to put your name on it. We will have an equal chance to see whom posterity decides to favour.

Do look around the room. I'll be able to study your face in different lights. Not much to see, though; I've cast the material world aside and live as simply as the fishermen of this island. I have some books, some clothes, my paints and a few pots and pans. Not that I cook much; there is a perfectly good bar in the village, and the widow who keeps it will prepare a meal for me whenever I like, which is most of the time. Don't look like that; she's fat, old and has a fearsome temper. You will stay there, if you insist on going ahead with this project. As you see, I am hardly in a position to offer you hospitality and wouldn't anyway. I have grown used to solitude, and now prefer it. I have only the one truckle bed, which you would find as uncomfortable as sleeping on the floor. Madame Le Gurun's accommodation will not be much better, but you will get a true taste of deep France to shock your delicate sensibilities. This is not Paris, nor Deauville nor yet Pau, I warn you.

I can see on your face that you are surprised, even a little disoriented by all this. What did you have in your mind, as you travelled to see me? A lovely *maison de maître*, nestling in the hills, at least. Servants, certainly. People of some sort—a *maire*, an *avocat*, a doctor to invite me to dinner. Surely your old friend would insist on some sort of society in which to bathe his ego, however provincial it might be? Did you think this poor benighted island was like Belle-Ile over there, that poets and playwrights came in the summer to preen themselves on my terrace? Could the man you knew in London exist without being surrounded by company?

And what do you find? Nothing. A dingy, smoke-filled house with the roof coming off—perfectly serviceable, though, I assure you. Scarcely any furniture. A painter dressed in rags, looking hardly better than a tramp, living like some hermit on a windswept, bare island inhabited only by a few hundred Breton fishermen and their families. I mean, how extreme!

You're right, of course, but what would be pretentious in Chelsea is perfectly acceptable here. What difference would it make how I dressed? No one ever sees me, except when I beg passage to go to Quiberon, and then I dress as fine as any country lawyer. I trim my beard—which you must admit is very fine and distracts attention from the ever-thinner hair on my head. And I struggle into my old suit with much wheezing; I have put on weight in the past few years as you see, and my clothes fit only with a protest. Still, I am elegant in comparison to most people in these parts, and with a straw hat on my head at its old jaunty angle, and with the walking stick that you gave me as a present, I believe I still cut a grand enough figure. I may be eccentric, but I do not want a reputation for such; it is the one way of attracting attention which I have always disdained. I need only one bed, one chair, one table, so that is all I have. The walls are bare; look out of the window and you have a finer sight than any painter has ever placed on a piece of canvas. And constantly changing, as well. The intensity and variety of the sea is extraordinary; there is no chance of ever getting bored with it, and I find even the greatest painting wearies me sooner or later. As for my own works, I know perfectly well what they look like, each and every one. I don't need to hang them up and look at them, and don't need anyone else to look, either.

Stop! Don't move! That will do; I want you to be comfortable, as I intend to keep you here for some time. I am out of practise, remember, and creaking bones go slower than well-exercised ones. I have mainly spent my time painting landscapes, and hills neither move nor talk back to you. Nor do they try to sneak into an elegant posture, or have a supercilious look on their faces. Remove both, if you please. I intend to paint you with grandeur, not as some simpering aesthete. A smirk is of its time. Solemnity is for eternity.

Let me explain my thinking. What I have decided to do— and I am not interested in your opinion on the matter—is a portrait in which a variation in light will show up different aspects of your character. Think of Monet. No, I haven't changed my mind; I still think he was not a good painter. But undoubtedly a great one, and as you know, I have never minded leaning on the great. So I'll need you morning, afternoon and evening, depending on where I am in my work. For an ordinary portrait, one glance is enough; for most sitters it is more than enough. A man of complexity requires more, and a poor painter like me needs all the help he can get. Perhaps Titian could communicate all levels at once, but he was a genius and I—as you once pointed out—am not. A hurtful comment, you know, until I recognised its truth. I discovered early on that I could always forgive you anything, as long as you told the truth. Then I learnt how to use that knowledge, and bend my skills to my limitations, and exceed both. Intelligence and craft, sometimes, can be an effective substitute for native ability.

I intend to cheat, mind you; my account of you is partly finished already. You remember, no doubt? The portrait I began in Hampshire in 1906? I brought it with me; my departure was not as sudden as it seemed. I gave myself more than enough time to pack and take with me the things I considered important. For some reason, your face was amongst all the other debris I felt I could not do without, even though it had been lying in my studio unfinished for three years. Every now and then, I take it out and look at it. About a year ago I finally got around to completing it, the first panel: *The Critic As He Was;* now I will begin on *The Critic As He Is.* One day, perhaps, *As He Will Be.* Past, present and future, all in one gorgeous trilogy.

So we will revisit Van Dyck together, you and I. You know what I mean, of course; the triple portrait of Charles I. An allusion, if you like, to your renowned connoisseurship. But not a pastiche; those pictures have the two outer pictures looking inwards, the king regards nothing but himself. The middle portrait stares out, calm and arrogant, not caring what the world sees or thinks. That would never do for a man like yourself. The critic must look outwards, all the time. Over your shoulder even, lest you miss some new fashion sneaking up from behind.

Do you remember when we saw that picture together? You took me along as part of my London education. I was in awe of you, even though I was already in my fumbling way a better painter than you could ever dream of becoming. But you had vast knowledge and a boundless self-confidence, and I wanted that from you, wanted to see how you did it. So I watched; you taught, and my dependency grew still greater. I didn't realise then that it was not something that could be mimicked. That assurance had deep roots that I could never grow for myself. That ability of yours never to doubt, never to hesitate about the correctness of your opinions, was part of your character, not mine.

Not mere arrogance, either. You had the right to your confidence, just as those colonial governors and members of Parliament have a right to their authority. You had spent years studying these pictures, while I merely had worked at painting some myself; immersed yourself in everything from Vasari to Morelli, while I was labouring away in a Glasgow drawing shop; travelled Europe from Hamburg to Naples before I had even left Scotland.

And I thought I could have all that merely by being around you for a few months. You never told me it was impossible. You never warned me and said, "I went to Winchester and Cambridge; I have known artists and writers, lords and ladies, all my life. I know Italy and France as well as I know my own country. You are a poor Scottish boy of no education and no connections, who has seen nothing but what I have shown you. We see and understand things differently, and always will. Find your own way, or you will only ever be ridiculous." Had you said that, I would not have believed you—at least not then. But it would have been the truth; you would have done your duty.

What is that you have so furtively popped into your mouth? A pill? Medicine? Are you ill? Let me see what you have in that bag. Goodness, even your maladies are fashionable! A weakness in the heart, I suppose. Do you need to lie down occasionally, become soporific and frail without these things? Have the vapours on a settee? Strange how this age has turned weakness into something attractive and interesting, decided that frailty and artistic judgement are two sides of the same thing. Like Beardsley and his tuberculosis, spluttering his contamination all over people at the dinner table. Would he have been taken so seriously had he been in robust good health and gone swimming in the ocean in December? I think not, somehow. Anyway, let me know if you feel like slipping off your chair into a stupor. If you are going to spoil the pose I would like a little advance warning.

By all means, pour a glass of water and eat your little pills. It is the wrong time of day for serious work in any case. Had you arrived on time, then maybe something might have been done today. But when were you ever on time? Making others wait is part of your manner. I didn't get out of bed until more than an hour after you were due. You weren't going to have me hanging around, working myself up into a bad mood on our first day. And I shall give Madame Le Gurun strict instructions that you are to be woken up at daybreak, and pushed out the door by six. For her, as for most of the people hereabouts, that is a long and decadent lie-in. The morning light is what I want for you, to start with. Clear and shadowless, with the freshness of dawn. Nothing is hidden, and the slight chill you get at this time of year stimulates the senses wonderfully. You will have the delight of walking across the island every morning at dawn, seeing the sea in its infinite variety. Then, later on, I think the evening, with long shadows accentuating that long nose of yours, the watchful look of slight malevolence you have sometimes, when you are briefly unaware that anyone is looking at you.

I have seen it many times. I particularly remember the first occasion. Do you want to hear? Why not? You have nothing better to do, after all, and although I allow myself to talk as much as I like while I work, it is not something I encourage in my sitters. It is, after all, how I created my reputation. Ah! A smile, if only a slight one. Please don't. Solemn, remember. What was the woman's name? Not that it matters. She'd married way above herself and was headachingly nervous.

She talked incessantly in a high, squeaky twitter, and eventually I had to finish quickly to avoid strangling her. I exhibited the portrait at the New English exhibition of 1903 with one of those silly academic titles. *Lost for Words,* I called it. My first success as a man of wit. It gained me some standing and reputation, and all for the small cost of humiliating a perfectly decent woman. I never apologised, not even when I came to regret it.

But that look of yours, the one I intend to go a-hunting for, that *particular* look I first noticed at Julien's *académie de peinture.* Hateful place; I learned nothing there at all, but it was good for the reputation, and I was very mindful of that. What painter could be taken seriously in London without having studied in Paris? So off we all trooped, me and Rothenstein and McAvoy and Connard and all the other hopefuls, and sat around and drew and painted and argued and damned all others for their mediocrity. Well, it was fun to live in poverty and be perpetually borrowing money off each other, and to dream of conquering the world, of striding into the new century as conquerors claiming our birthright. We came back to London so full of ourselves, with such hopes! Maybe that was the point of it. But I certainly didn't learn to paint there. Just to work quickly in a dark and smoky room with an incessant din all around me. I learned to live in a crowd and maintain my sense of self. I learned that I'd have to be detached if I was ever to achieve anything at all. And I learned how cruel is the world of art; how much like a jungle, where only the most powerful survive. A harsh and surprising lesson, as I had been used to the gentler atmosphere of drunken working men in Glasgow, whose only violence is to beat each other senseless on a Saturday night.

I remember when Evelyn first joined us in 1898, after I'd been there for two years and was already beginning to think of going to see whether I would survive in the great cauldron of the London painting world. She didn't come for the life class, of course; women weren't allowed into that. For one of the general lessons in perspective, an arrangement of dying flowers in a vase, an old jar, a hammer, all arranged quite indecorously. Curious spectacle, all those budding young revolutionaries, peering earnestly at that homely arrangement like a bunch of polite schoolboys. And then this girl comes in, and everyone sniggers. She was so young, so innocent-looking and so—prim. The sort who lives with her mother, drinks sherry once a month and is in bed by half past nine every night. Not the sort of woman you would want as a subject for a painting, unless you have a yen to depict the frail and delicate; although once I looked closer I thought maybe you could do something interesting with those pale cheeks, the thin hair pulled tightly into an unflattering bun at the nape of the neck, the slightly hunched pose, as if she were trying to hide her small breasts, pretend they were not there. She looks around, arranges herself, says good morning in a quiet, nervous voice, then begins. We all crowd round after a bit, to see the polite bit of feminine nonsense she had produced, and I saw that expression on your face.

You had come to take me to dinner, and were waiting with unaccustomed patience for me to clean myself up enough to look respectable. Normally it was the other way round, with me waiting like a young girl for her first beau. I'd only known you for a month or so then, and was already captivated. A chance, overheard remark in a museum, and you came up to me and invited me for a drink. The Café de l'Opéra! Champagne! Brilliant conversation, so worldly and knowing. You were already known, and had started writing reviews of Paris exhibitions for the newspapers in London. Were the editor of an advanced journal with no circulation, someone who turned up at parties and dinners. Had a reputation for—something, although no-one really knew what. Yet you pursued me, initiated the friendship and cultivated it. You chose me to be your friend! You singled me out, paid attention to me, began my education. I was twenty-seven, but so inexperienced of this new world I wished to enter I'm sure I seemed much younger. You were near thirty already, but almost jaded from having seen so much.

I think the others laughed at me behind my back, but I didn't care. I wore my adoration, my reverence, like a badge of pride. "William says . . ." "William thinks . . ." "William and I . . ." Heavens, but I must have been ridiculous. You encouraged it, flattered and cajoled. "Don't worry about the others. An artist like yourself . . ." "You have something special; real ability . . ." All those phrases; I lapped them up, wanted more, wanted you to say them again and again. It was like bathing in milk. And I didn't realise how much I filled a need in you: everything was fresh for me; you had seen everything before, many times over. With me in tow you could catch some of the excitement of discovery and feel the joy of novelty once more. I think it is why you so earnestly advocate the new in art. You are constantly in search of something to excite you and stir an enthusiasm that a too-fortunate education has snatched from your grasp.

No-one had ever taken me seriously before. You were the first not to regard me as skilled only in self-deception. You patronised me, of course, but then you patronised everyone. But even I realised that you liked to be around when I saw something for the first time, discovered a painter I had never heard of, gazed with wonder on a masterpiece you had known all your life. You could tell me everything about the artist, dissect his skill and turn his genius into words. But you couldn't be frozen in amazement, couldn't tremble with emotion. I provided that for you, and in return you gave me an education. Until you came along, I was sustained only by a deep-seated Scottish doggedness, but I knew already it wasn't going to be enough. I loved you for that, always will. Because you were right, after all: I am a good artist.

I threw myself into my work under your tutelage, labouring all hours of the day and night to make myself better, laying my improvements before you like a faithful dog coming back to his master with a stick. And I did get better, improved in ways I scarcely thought possible; I learned to take risks, not to be safe and hide behind my skill. Oh, bliss it was! I still look back on those evenings we spent together as the happiest part of my life, and I wanted it to go on forever. I didn't want to get to know you any better; didn't want to think about the shadows and the subtleties. But innocence is only pleasurable because it is transient.

How is it that expressions change? I have spent years looking at people's faces, and it is still a mystery to me. A minuscule, immeasurable movement of an eyebrow in relation to the eye and nose; a scarcely discernible tightening or loosening of the muscles in cheek and neck; the barest tremor on the lips; a shine in the eyes. But we know the eyes do not change; the most significant manifestation of emotion is pure illusion. And this fractional shifting is all that distinguishes contempt from respect, love from anger. Some people are crude; their faces can be read by anyone. Some are more subtle, and only those close to them can read the face correctly. Some are incomprehensible even to themselves.

It has taken me years to unpick the expression on your face when you looked at Evelyn's work that day in the atelier. I sometimes think my entire career, my life, even, could be cast as the quest to decipher that look, to peel away layer after layer, to plunge down into your mind and piece together the fragmentary emotions and responses that I saw but could not understand. I managed it eventually; I will tell you how soon enough.

So the expression was obscure, but the response was not. That was as clear as a bell. A polite dismissal. Not even contempt. It carried weight, I followed you, but not so far as to make some comment; even then I could see something of myself in her. And I was not comfortable. Because my own immediate reaction had been different—the brief start that comes into the mind when faced with something unexpected and surprising. I could have dismissed that easily, of course; but it was echoed by the momentary hesitation I noticed in you; a sliver of time between your looking and your response.

That's what I want in this picture, the one I have been carefully sketching out all this while. I want that look, that penetration. I want that ability to see reflected back on the viewer, want the person looking at this portrait to think that it is he who is being assessed, not the other way round. And unless you manage to give it to me, old friend, I'll have to try and conjure it up from my memory. No-one will understand but me, of course; it may be that it will all go down as merely a piece of bad painting, or be overlooked entirely. It doesn't matter; this is not just a public portrait. It is also a private matter, between you and me. So that you understand my understanding, if you follow me.

You see, the problem I have at the moment is that you have grown just a touch sleek in the last few years. I hadn't expected that before you arrived, so I am having to rethink my approach. You've become a bit *too* self-confident, somewhat priggish. All those years back, there was a faint anxiety to your features. It made you more human, more complex at the same time that it made you more difficult and—let us not beat about the bush—more prickly. Your snobbishness, your arrogance, your ambition were all nearer the surface then, and even though they are not normally appealing qualities, they made you a more attractive person, and certainly an easier one to paint. Now years of success have worn all that away; I see none of it any more. But it is still there, somewhere, and I intend to bring it out. I know you haven't really changed.

At the moment you look merely sardonic, detached. No good at all. You've ruined my morning. We will stop here. No, I've no idea what you should do for the rest of the day; that's your problem. I suggest a walk. You have too much of the urban about you; it makes you pale and rather lifeless—desiccated, even. Fresh air and exercise would be very much better for you than those nasty little pills. Besides, there are some things to see around here if you look; they are careless of their history in these parts and leave it lying around in the most surprising places. I like that tendency in them; they are concerned with the present, and feel no need to preserve and catalogue every last stone of their past. They have been futurists for generations. The avant-garde can tell them nothing they do not already know.

I admit Houat is not much to look at, at first sight; it

doesn't yield up its charms easily. There's nothing for a man schooled in Gainsborough, who knows of the sublime beauty of the Alpine landscape, the wooded gentleness of Suffolk, or expects his Campagna to be peopled with besporting nymphs and shepherds. There are no mountains, no woods. Scarcely even any trees. You have to look to see the clumps of wild carnations, the yellow of the broom, or the jasmine. The variety of grasses, each with a subtly different colour. All these things need to be studied, but above all you have to study the sea, which is the alpha and omega of this place, its definition and cause. The colours, the tones, the shapes of the sea in its different guises are all the scenery you need; it is an endless show, and can conjure up every emotion and mood. I recommend a closer look; walk along Treac'h er Goured—the whole island, after all, is only a couple of miles long; even you could manage it—and find the holy fountain. Sit by it while you smell the wind and feel the sun. Stay long enough and you will begin to see what I mean, perhaps. Go to the church in the village, take a walk along the beach, the cliffs, and look out over the sea. Consider the fort overlooking the island, the stonework of the quay. There are menhirs and dolmens here, although such echoes of a pagan past are supposed to have been destroyed.

What more could any reasonable man want? There is enough for a lifetime of contemplation. Tell me what you think tomorrow.

And while you are at it, I will cast an eye over my morning's labour and, no doubt, find it wanting. At the moment, though, I'm not displeased with my efforts. I've caught that way your chin rises above the horizontal and gives you the air of aloofness and superiority you use so well. But not too much; don't worry. I haven't yet descended into caricature. And no, you can't see it. This isn't a collaboration. I paint; you sit. When you are in that chair, you are stripped of your expertise, of your taste and discernment. Your opinion is of no more value to me than that of the old peasant I sketched last month. You are defenceless until I am finished.

Don't look petulant; it is only a passing torment you have to endure. Painters have to live with the opinions of others forever, and so we try to ignore them as much as possible, like these islanders who do not notice the stone memorials to the hardships they have witnessed. Think of the cruelties you have inflicted on others with your pen—for the most part justified I am sure, but no less hurtful for that—and consider how petty my revenge will be. Besides, I have to be true to what I see; I cannot be too harsh on you when I trace the line of that chin. I remember too well how it made me laugh, how I flung myself into agreement with its disdainful movements.

Shut the door when you go out. The wind is getting up and I don't want my papers blowing about.

DO YOU KNOW, after you left yesterday I spent the next hour walking about this little room—which I grandly call my studio—cursing you? And myself, for not throwing you out the moment you set foot over the threshold. Why did you suggest I paint your portrait? I know the reasons you insinuated in your letter, of course—expressed delicately and gravely, you felt I needed help. Needed to feel you still loved me. That you didn't resent the way I abandoned you and went off without a word. A portrait would perhaps restore my self-confidence, and give me some much-needed income. A picture of you at some exhibition would be a fine way of advertising my continued existence, maybe even ease my return to London. Is that it? I am grateful; touched. It has always been your worst characteristic, to bestow generous aid and ask nothing obvious in return. No wonder so many people distrust you. I can see you talking it over with your wife, as she sits on the sofa and reads, you at your desk by the big window. Proof-reading a review? Working up a lecture? Are you still working on that book you started in Paris? You look up. "I've been thinking about Henry quite a lot recently. I really think I should see if I can help him a little. . . ."

And she smiles. She had a lovely smile. "Such an awkward man! You know I never really took to him. But I know he is an old friend of yours, my dear. . . ."

You go on: "What about writing to him and seeing if he'll have another go at a portrait? I hear he is not at all well. His last few letters have been rambling, almost incoherent, so I'm told. That way I'll be able to find out how he is. . . ."

So your excellent wife—a fine woman, who has never directly denied you anything—gives her assent, and you write to me. Maybe I am inventing; but I'm sure I am close.

But that is not it, is it? I have been here near four years now, with not a peep from you before. If you wanted to send me money, there are easy enough ways of doing it. And no amount of friendship would make you spend more than ten minutes on this island unless there was some compelling reason. People can change, but not that much. You get faint crossing Hyde Park. Nature has never been one of your loves. So what is it that makes you need to sit in my presence for days on end? What is it that you are after, that you evidently cannot ask me directly? That is the way you draw people in, is it not? Sit silently, until they speak to fill up the silence; give little away yourself while the other person reveals their soul?

You see, your very presence takes me back into the past and wakes up all sorts of memories I had forgotten about for years, which have not troubled me for a long time. I got no work done whatsoever after you left, and had recourse in the early evening to that wine which you find so revolting. I drank far too much of it, had only an omelette for dinner; I didn't want to go to Mère Le Gurun for fear you would be there. The prospect of an evening's conversation with you made me feel perfectly sick, so I stayed put and made myself feel ill all on my own. I slept badly. I haven't really slept well for years now. Not since I left England. Some nights are better than others, but last night I scarcely slept at all, despite the pharmacopoeia of potions I have in my little cupboard. I am in a bad mood, mainly because of my ageing stomach, which I find can take less and less of any sort of ill treatment. The man who once used to go for days without sleep in a frenzy of work is no more. Dead, my friend, and buried; only a shade remains, which needs an early night and cannot take too much wine.

I grant that there are some questions to be answered.

How is it that an artist in his prime, nearing the peak of his career, should act in such a foolish way? He has income, some small renown and (even better) reputation. He has just taken part in one of the most important exhibitions ever to be seen in the country, is at the vanguard of the artistic revolution sweeping the world. He has achieved, nearly, what he has aimed at all his life. From near poverty in Scotland, then time as a jobbing illustrator for scruffy magazines and penny dreadfuls in London, scrimping and saving to go to Paris, and finally the goal is at hand. Then suddenly—pop!— off he goes. Packs his bags and says farewell to more than twenty years of struggle and hard work. Tells no-one where he is for some time, refuses to answer letters. Why? There is no insanity in the family, is there? Both his parents were well-nigh teetotal, were they not? If he has some horrible disease, better, surely, that he stay in London and get proper medical treatment? What is the cause of this behaviour? What did he do that makes him flee the country like some murderer on the run?

There are limits to eccentricity, after all. Behaving outrageously is conventional, necessary for any painter wishing to be taken seriously these days. But this is beyond outrageous. It is offensive. The whole point of running off to the continent in a fit of aesthetic pique is to come back again, so others may revel in the deed, glory in the flouting of convention, draw strength from the shock and disapproval of others. To disappear completely, send back no pictures to advertise your continued existence, is different; it implies a disdain for all those artists in Chelsea and beyond, and few people can forgive being disdained. Makes them look at their metropolitan lives and wonder. What's wrong with being here? Should we be doing that too? Or it makes people suspicious, makes them gossip.

You want an explanation. You have a right to know. Well, we shall see; I think you may know the reasons as well as I do. As my painting progresses, perhaps mutual understanding will emerge as well as a portrait. I have been waiting nearly four years for you to ask; you can wait a few days for my answer.

Sit, then; the light is good and I'm often at my best when in an ill-humour. No, no, no. You know better than that. Both arms on the chair, head against the rest; you are meant to look senatorial, the Roman of old, an imposing figure of authority. Don't you remember? Or did your dinner have a similar effect on you as on me that you slump there like an empty paper bag? That's better. Now keep still, for pity's sake.

Memories? Oh yes. Both good and bad, I assure you.

Worst of all, you brought out feelings of regret, for the first time since I came here. But then, you always had that effect on me, so why should it be any different now? I started thinking about what might have been, had I stayed in London, had I cultivated people properly, had I stayed in the fight, had I got married. I saw the career ahead of me, culminating in a large house in Holland Park or Kensington, revered by my many pupils, rather than forgotten and living in total isolation. Too late now. Now I would have the reputation of being unreliable, an unsafe pair of hands. How many commissions do you think I abandoned when I left? At least a dozen, most of them paid for. And I doubt that what I paint these days would find much favour. Too eccentric, too strange.

It could have been different, as you know. It was within my grasp; all I had to do was keep in favour with people like you, produce works that were suitably advanced but not too daring that no-one would buy them. That is why I can indulge in regret. You can't regret a fantasy; only a real opportunity lost can produce that sort of wistfulness. Would success have been so delicious as it seemed when I thought about it late last night in my bed? Probably not; I tasted enough of it to get the bitterness on my tongue, the dry feeling in my mouth when I complimented ugly old women for the sake of their husbands' wallets, or made polite conversation to dealers interested only in the difference between buying and selling prices. I knew the vulnerability of the successful with those beneath, eager to tear them down and feast on their entrails.

Did we not do that, you and I? Would I have been spared in my turn? I think not. It is the cycle of the generations, played out in every species that walks the face of the earth. The rise of the young, the tearing down of the old. Again and again. Was I supposed to sleepwalk meekly through a play where the script was already written, on which I could have no influence? We sat long hours in Paris bars and London pubs, sneering at the likes of Bouguereau and Herkomer and Hunt, deriding their pomposity, the prostitution of their skills into sterile emblems for the bourgeoisie—those were the glorious, rolling phrases, were they not? How good they made us feel. But what would those below say about me now? What are they called again? Vorticists, Cubists, Futurists or some such? Too weird even for you, I imagine. Sentimental, I think, might be one word for the sort of stuff I was producing in London. Prettified, perhaps; insincere would wound because it would be true. And no doubt a whole raft of other insults I cannot even imagine. Who knows what sins we committed in our turn when we cast our elders into the darkness and trampled so gleefully on their reputations?

We weren't really very good, you know. Think of all those acres of canvas we churned out when we came back from Paris, all that semi-digested Impressionism. We got rid of the wistful peasants and the studies of girls knitting, true enough; but we replaced them with unending landscapes painted in muted greens and browns. Thousands of them. Didn't really matter if it was Cumbria or Gloucestershire or Brittany, they all looked pretty much the same. I don't know why English painters love brown so much. It's not as if it is so much cheaper than any other colour. We learned from the Impressionists only how to produce pictures safe enough to hang on the parlour wall, next to the engraving of the Queen and the needlepoint made by Granny when she was young.

It is the violence these new people bring to their work which interests me; what they produce may be revolting, incompetent, the antithesis of real art; they may be frauds and fools. Who knows? But they tap into the violence of men's souls like the first roll of thunder on a summer's day. They have extended their emotional range into areas we never thought of. There was nothing of that in our work. We challenged those old men in so many ways, but our notion of violence was still heroic. General Wolfe capturing Quebec, Napoleon crossing the Alps. No blood, no death and no cruelty. We produced studies of sunlight on cathedral walls and thought that was revolutionary enough. I could have led the way, you know.

Anyway, I decided not to wait for my inevitable eclipse. I would not be a sitting target. I retreated, packed up, came here; foreswore the knighthood, the obituary in *The Times*, the commemorative retrospective at the Royal Academy. I did not wish others to destroy my reputation, so I did it myself, before they could strike me down. At least I would deprive them of the pleasure. Cowardice, you may have thought at the time. I prefer to think of it as being acute. What soldier stands and waits to be overcome by a superior force? Better to get out of the way.

And bide my time. My renunciation was tactical, not mystical. I do not yearn for obliteration; my opinion of my work is too high for that. True, the wait will be long, but I am not concerned with my reputation during my life. Even had I achieved immense fame, I knew it would evaporate soon enough. I am after a bigger prize than that. Far bigger.

You think I am deranged, that the years of loneliness and isolation have finally tipped me over into an insane self-importance. Ah, but you will see, when I have finished this painting. You will see.

I suppose I'd better tell you my secret; you'll find it out on your own, and I don't want that smirk of yours to appear without being summoned by me. I have taken to going to church. Not just for the aesthetics of it all, either. I do the whole thing. Communion, confession, everything. A good Catholic I have become—me, brought up in the Church of Scotland, which abominates all things papist. If you want to break with your past, exterminate history beyond all hope of recovery, there is no better way of accomplishing it than a good conversion, I find. I think it was the discipline of it which attracted me. I was, after all, living in this house on my own, without any attachments, and I needed to give some form to the week. You'll see that it has influenced my painting considerably. I'm now more than conversant with the sufferings of the martyrs, for the local priest is very keen on such things, and likes to go on about it in his sermons. A man for miracles as well, which I find refreshing these days, when everyone seeks an explanation and refuses to believe anything which cannot be made rational.

He has undertaken my education in matters religious, and gives me readings to ponder after my confessions. He has a predilection for the old Celtic saints, coming as he does from sturdy Breton stock, and I find that they appeal to me greatly as well. A few months ago I read about Saint Coloman, who was accused of being a traitor for some reason and killed. He was hanged, and his body was left on the gibbet, uncorrupted, for eighteen months. I think the point of the story is that it was only his death which sanctified him; before that he had been nothing extraordinary, yet the hate of others turned him into something not even crows dared defile. We are a long way from Good Works and the teaching of the kirk here. Do you think that was why the good father chose that for my bedside reading? Or perhaps there was something else in his mind. Perhaps I was meant to think about those who killed him; they were all drowned.

If I let you see what I am doing here, you would see instantly how Catholic my eyes have become under the influence of such teaching. There you sit on your chair, which I am subtly transforming into a throne. Your pose is imperious, you are more than a mere critic writing for newspapers and fashionable magazines. I seek to approach truth through subtle flattery, you see. I will not short-change you; I have given my word on that. No mere journalist, then, but something more. You will have the pose of a pope, as painted by

Velázquez, to remind everyone of the power that people like yourself wield in our modern world. You command, and it comes to pass. You lift your finger and a reputation is made, shake your head and the hopes nurtured for years in the ateliers, worked for and so desperately desired, are dashed forever. So, you do not move armies, do not wreak destruction on faraway lands like our politicians and generals. You are far more powerful than that, are you not? You change the way people think, shape the way they see the world. A great power, wielded without check or hindrance. A despotism of the arts, in which you are high priest of the true and the beautiful. Very much like the Pope in your own way, and in my fashion so will I honour you.

But the church and myself? Yes; I am serious. I have always believed in sin, you know, my Scottish forebears gave me that if nothing else. But I always found Scottish sin so unsatisfying. There is so much of it you can't really distinguish between any of its wonderful varieties. Playing cards on a Sunday, drinking alcohol for more than medical necessity, seducing your neighbour's wife, murder—it is all one and the same, sin which condemns you to eternal torment. Wake up, get out of bed, go downstairs and have breakfast, and already your soul is lost. So why not murder someone as well?

You're doomed before you're even out of the cradle anyway. Down here they are more subtle in the matter. They have big sins and little sins, sins mortal and sins minor; you are not thrust into hellfire without any say in the matter. You have to earn damnation.

A God like that I have time for. We get along, and as He has made my life so much more interesting, I find I can believe in Him a little. So I go to Mass, and sit in rapture with the fishermen and their wives, bathe in the odour of haddock and sanctity, and confess four times a year. I find I have little to own up to these days, so I have to go back over the years, clearing away the backlog. I fear the priest groans when he sees me coming, as he knows he's going to get another chapter of autobiography which will have him crouched in his little confessional for hours. He suspects me of enthusiasm, which is itself a sin.

On the other hand, he cannot say that I do not have a wondrous variety of faults to own up to. I keep him entertained; occasionally I hear an intake of breath, and I feel him half-smiling in shock, and, I suspect, with more than a little envy. You must meet him, by the way. I don't mean that because you will enjoy the experience, although he is pleasant enough. Or because he is the high point of social life on the island, even though that is true as well. You *must* meet him:

it is an absolute obligation. His power in his domain is greater than that of the Pope in what is left of his. This island of Houat is a theocracy. I do not joke. The priest is deputy mayor, but ensures a nonentity has the official role so that everything is done his way. He is head of the fishing syndicate. The magistrate. The headmaster of the school. His nuns control the electric telegraph, and he has only recently given up control of the alcohol supply. You do not annoy Father Charles. Not if you want to stay on this island. He is monarch, head of the judiciary and God's representative on earth, all incarnate in the same small man. And he has the only good cook on the island. Benevolent, but in his sphere as autocratic as you are in yours. You must go and see him; if you do not, he will come and see you, and that would be impolite. Do please try to make yourself agreeable, for my sake. None of your witty cosmopolitan repartee, if you don't mind. He is a proud man, very protective of his subjects who, you should know, do not object to their subjection. Were it not Father Charles, it would be someone else, who might not be so enthusiastic at keeping the French at bay.

This is the man who has taken your place as my guide and confessor. I did my best to enjoy my sins, but I find atoning for them is more pleasurable. Do you know, he once called me a libertine? A marvellously *ancien régime* term, which I was quite taken by. I came back home and immediately sketched myself as Hogarth's rake, soaked in debauchery in my studio, with my two favourite models draped all over me. I burnt it, though, as I didn't manage to put in any severity, only nostalgia, which wasn't proper. You can't be forgiven unless you truly regret—that's one of the rules, apparently—and it was clear evidence that my regret was far from total.

Besides, it was a lie; my sins were never so elaborate. Even when my very soul is at stake I can't resist the tendency to overpaint the subject. It is a weakness you pointed out to me years ago, and the Lord knows how hard I have tried to rein myself in, to stick to facts, to obey the law as laid down both by God and William Nasmyth. But I never succeed for long. Sooner or later, I heighten the colour, clutter the image or add an extra model to my memories.

JACKY WAS ONE of the figures in my sketch, of course, always my real favourite as a subject. She was so disgusting, so common, so vulgar, you couldn't help admiring her. And a brilliant model, as well. A body like Aphrodite, a face like the

Virgin and an ability to stand still for hours in any pose you cared to ask for. I've always preferred women on the Rubens scale, myself. None of these skinny Botticelli types for me, all points and angles. With Jacky you got the opulence of form, rounded and full, set off by a flawless skin that was almost like marble. She was the personification of fecundity itself; everything about her was sensual, fleshy. What else could anyone want?

I imagined initially she was thinking when she sat for me, but eventually I concluded there was nothing inside at all. A complete blank. Time had no meaning. A minute, an hour, a day, it was all the same to her. She had nothing better to do, and so she simply sat still. I think that was what she did when she was on her own; having me pay her to do what came naturally was an extra bonus. But when she did talk, my goodness! The contrast between that angelic expression and dull mouth was remarkable. "So I said to her, I said, if you think I'm going to give you tuppence-ha'penny for that, you got another think coming. I told her straight and do you know what she said to me. . . ." On and on she would drone, giving details about the price of tomatoes or cloth or how she burned some cake, or couldn't find a stocking, until your head was spinning and you wanted to jump out of the window just to get away from her. I always thought it most perplexing, because I still, somewhere, held on to the old notion that character is reflected in the face. Not in the case of our Jacky, and the discovery fast killed off any desire. You could ask her to do anything, and she would meekly obey, but it was like making love to a cardboard box; movement but no passion, not even the pretence of any engagement. Just the same vacant stare. I knew, of course, that she had alternative sources of income, that she "entertained a gentleman," as she put it in a show of primness—I always suspected that somewhere in there was a lower-middle-class housewife, who dreamed, perhaps, of her parlour and of washing day. I do not think the gentleman in question could have been greatly entertained. Nor did I wonder who the poor soul might be; just felt sorry for him.

A pity she went and killed herself, though; she deprived the world of many a fine picture by her selfishness. I never would have thought it possible, until I read about it in the paper. Part-time prosititute dragged from river, the papers said. She deserved a better memorial than that, despite her many failings. The best model in London, in my opinion, but stupid. Very stupid. Imagine killing herself just because she got herself pregnant! Who would have thought she was even capable of feeling shame? Let alone acting on it in such an extreme way. Very perplexing. She was silly when alive, and died as she had lived, it seems.

Ah! Such an impenetrable face you have, my friend! Such control. You are a painter's nightmare, you know. It was something I once admired greatly. The stoicism of the English gentleman is a wonderful thing, unless you are trying to capture it on canvas, because emotions bounce off it and never reveal themselves. Tell you something shocking or wondrous, insult you or compliment you, and that same inscrutable expression comes back. It is like trying to peer through a dirty window: you do not see true, and end up seeing only your own faint reflection instead. That will not do. You must show some strong emotion for me before you leave or I will throw down my brushes and stamp out in a painterly rage. Haven't had one of those for years.

Curiously, Evelyn took to Jacky. I passed her on when she came back to London in 1902. She needed a model, and eventually Jacky became her one and only sitter. It was a strange conjunction. Each supplied a lack in the other, I suppose; Evelyn must have liked Jacky's simplicity, the domesticity of her mind, the vacuity of her tastes. Perhaps she wanted a refuge from all that aestheticism, needed an occasional antidote to the high seriousness of creation. Can you understand such a thing, William? Might it ever appeal to you? And Jacky responded to something in Evelyn; her independence and her silence, perhaps. The inner strength that belied the feeble frame. Or perhaps she saw more than I did, and realised how very fragile she truly was, and responded to her courage. She was laughed at, I know, when people like myself—who thought the low made suitable subjects for art but not for conversation—saw them together in the street. Arm in arm, sometimes. Friends. Not artist and model, or mistress and servant. There was a certain lack of decorum in being so familiar; a bit like taking the parlourmaid out to a restaurant.

And how they could spend so much time together was a mystery, especially as Jacky would scold her on occasion like some old shrew. I wouldn't have put up with being talked to in such a way by a mere model, but Evelyn didn't seem to mind, even showed signs of being properly apologetic. She found friendship in all sorts of odd places, and never really enjoyed the company of other artists. She was one of those people who could winkle out something interesting in almost anyone, if she chose. I thought that with Jacky the effort must have been almost superhuman, but it never looked that way when I saw them together. She seemed far more relaxed than ever she was with me. Not that I thought about it then.

I need no models now; I haven't painted any woman under forty for some time. They guard their womenfolk carefully here, and it is a small island. Besides, I don't find all
these lacy coifs particularly appealing, and they don't go
about with their heads uncovered. Nor, for the most part,
are they particularly appealing subjects, unless you like to
paint weather-beaten faces and the effects of back-breaking
work or scant food. Not the sort of subject matter that usually appeals, and they are not open-faced; you would have to
know them much better to penetrate their minds and turn
them into something worth looking at. Still, beauty can
flourish in even the most inhospitable terrain. There is one
girl I would love to paint; she has the eyes of the devil. But
we have done no more than exchange glances over an ex-
panse of church. I fascinate her, I know. I am to her what you
were for me: a new world, full of opportunities, offering
everything she wants and cannot win by herself unaided.
She wants to leave this island, to see and be different things.
She dreams at night of what it must be like, to be something
other than she is. She longs for freedom, and is hated for it by
many on this island. Her desires have made her difficult and
unsympathetic. It will eat away at that beauty soon enough.

If I intervened, her fate would change: whatever happened, she would go, would not marry the honest fisherman

who is her destiny, would not be aged before her time by hardship and pregnancy. Lord only knows how she would end up. But high or low, part of her wants to take the chance, to roll the dice. Anything but what is mapped out for her here. If only I would force her hand. Goodness, I see the temptation! But I won't; it is not for me to change her future. All she has to do is get on the boat and not come back. It's simple. If you change someone's life you have a responsibility to them forever; it is a heavy burden which you must not shirk. Do you not agree, William?

I have painted one portrait, though. Still life might be a better term. It's unfinished, like most of my work these days. But not through laziness; it cannot be completed. About a year ago, a boy was washed up at the place called Treac'h Salus, a fine sandy beach, about twenty minutes' walk from here. No-one knew who he was; not from this island certainly. Perhaps he'd been swept off a fishing boat in a storm the week before, but no-one had heard of such a thing. Perhaps he was a cabin boy on one of the passing steam ships, a stowaway, even. Enquiries were made, but he came from the sea—that was all anyone ever discovered. Those who know such things thought he'd been in the water a week or so, not much longer. I was having a morning walk when I saw the small group of islanders gathered around him in the distance;

there was something calm, reverential, about their pose; they were praying. You remember Millet's *Angelus*? The way the woman's head inclines to the ground, the way the man fiddles nervously with his hat, both lost in thought? The intensity of prayer depicted so simply and effectively?

My curiosity disturbed them as I approached over the sand, but I could not keep away; I needed to see what was producing that perfect pose. My reaction was quite different to theirs. They were reflective; I was fascinated. They were resigned; I was excited, stimulated. The brilliant colours of decay, the complex bundle of angles and curves on the twisted body, half-eaten and swollen. The green tint, reflecting purple and red in the sun that crept over an exposed leg, so recently young and strong. The way the majesty of the human form, God's image, could be reduced so easily by the sea to the obscene and grotesque. And the eye—one only, for the other had been eaten out of its socket. One eye was preserved, a pale sky blue shining like hope in that jumble of mouldy, stinking carcass. It still had personality and life, something which seemed almost amused by its predicament. And not fearful or distressed; perfectly calm, almost serene. An echo of the soul which survived despite everything that had happened. I could see it watching me, seeing how I would react.

Haunting. Literally so, because I could think of nothing else for days; I felt I knew it, had seen it looking at me before. I came back in the afternoon with a sketchbook, but the disapproval would have been so intense it wasn't worth trying to settle down. And for some reason I could not draw it properly without actually being there. All I could get down was that eye, which drowned out the rest of the scene like a brilliant light in darkness. Even though the image was fixed in my mind, the composition just so, the rest of the boy kept slipping away from me.

They buried him next day in the grim little graveyard, with a full funeral as if he had been one of their own. No small thing, that; funerals are expensive and these people have little enough to spare. But he could so easily have been one of their own children. A touching ceremony, really. Stark and austere like their own lives. The congregation gathered in the churchyard overlooking the sea, a genuine, heartfelt grief for someone they had never known, and never even suspected existed. They are good people, truly they are, though your expression as you listen to my tale shows how worthless they are to you.

One curious thing did happen a few days later, which even you might find intriguing. Maybe not. But the police heard about it and came over from Quiberon to find out what they could, and were properly cross that the boy had been buried already. Even threatened to dig him up again, although the priest soon put paid to that idea. The curiosity was that, to a man and a woman, they refused to say anything—not where the boy was found, nor what they did with him, nor any suspicions they might have had about who he was. They closed ranks completely, and responded to all questions with a sullen, stubborn silence. The boy was theirs, now. This was their business. Their obstinacy when confronted with anything to do with the outside world is extraordinary.

It brought back an old fascination of mine that had been lingering in the back of my mind for years. Do you remember those Sunday morning expeditions we used to do together in Paris? I found them so wonderful, getting up early, meeting in a café for some bread and coffee, then off for a day of talk and art. A close friendship, as close as it can be. My education, of more use to me in many ways than any time I spent in school or atelier. We saw Puvis de Chavannes in the Pantheon, and argued long whether his vast canvasses of saints were genius or mediocrity, triumph or disaster. I still haven't made up my mind, but I have a love for them because they are forever associated with the bliss of friendship and the joy of experience. We had the whole of the Louvre at our disposal, medieval wall paintings, Renaissance architecture, the sculptures of Houdon and Rodin; we saw churches and monuments, art modern and ancient. Studied Italian paintings and German prints together, ate and drank and walked. We sat in parks and dusty squares, walked by rivers and canals until the light faded, and still we went on talking. I remember the way you would stab the air with your finger to make a point as you marched along, the way you collapsed on a park bench and fanned yourself with a guidebook as you finished some wordy peroration about the use of public sculpture. The way you could recite poetry at the drop of a hat in your perfect French to illustrate some painting or panorama. The way you could turn anything into the subject for a lecture.

I came back from these outings exhausted, but unable to sleep, my head spinning with all I'd seen. And, of course, went over everything we had talked about. Had I said something stupid? Of course I had, many times over; so had you, but with such confidence no-one dared call it so. That was one of the things I learned; one of the most important things. But even then I think the seeds of our divergence were germinating; I remember a brief flutter of slight annoyance—swiftly suppressed—when you made some sneering remark about Boucher. Well, alright, not to everyone's taste, all those silly women dressed up as shepherdesses with those bouffant wigs perched on their heads. But look at the way the man painted! He could do anything; I couldn't believe it when I first saw them. That didn't matter to you at all, and maybe you were right. But you didn't see the man's sense of humour. Do you think he didn't know he was making these grand aristocrats look faintly absurd? Didn't you realise that was the point? No; humour was never your strong point. It was all too serious for you. Playfulness has always been absent in your life.

I remember the trip to Saint-Denis best of all, the great cathedral with the sepulchres of the kings in that grimy industrial suburb. It was one of those revelatory moments that come only rarely in a life, all the more so for being so very unexpected. Particularly Louis XII and his queen, those statues; showing both of them in their full glory, regal and powerful, and underneath as corpses, withered, naked and disgusting. As you are, so were we; as we are, so will you be. No sentimentality or hiding. No black crêpe or fine words to hide the reality. These people were able to confront the inevitable full on, and show that even kings must rot. It is our final destination, and something artists have shied away from for generations. We are young and agile; established and comfortable; dead and decayed. Hope, fear and peace. There are only three ages of man, not seven. I am painting the second now.

My failure with that boy on the beach, the most recent, annoyed me because the sculptors in that cathedral had succeeded. I could not understand it. It was a simple enough task, after all; a still-life composition no more complex than an arrangement of artefacts at Julien's *académie*. But I failed; all I managed was a bundle of shapeless rags, a sentimental, incoherent mess. It was little better than the sort of thing I would have knocked out for the *Evening Post*. "Mystery death of boy on beach." Two paragraphs, page four, illustrated with a grotesque sketch by myself, printed in two garish colours—three if it was sufficiently horrible.

It festered; I am not used to such setbacks. Normally my technique would have sustained me, and allowed me to produce something tolerable enough to revolt the general public. But I no more wanted something accomplished than I wanted something sanitised and artistic. D'you remember that appalling painting by Wallis in the Tate, *The Death of Chatterton*? Pretty young poet lies sprawled in an elegant pose across the bed after taking arsenic. Ha! That's not what you look like if you swallow arsenic! You're covered in filth, you stink, you lie crouched on the floor from the agony, your face screwed up, hideously disfigured as the poison eats away your intestines. You don't look as though you've just dropped off for a nap after too many cucumber sandwiches. But he couldn't paint that. That wouldn't have made people think sentimental tripe about doomed artists dying before their time. That's what I wanted to get away from, and not by painting landscapes or the poor enjoying themselves at the music hall. Real death—which is the stuff of life, after all. I know; I did quite a few suicides when I worked for those magazines. And murders and hangings. But it was always just work, and I only ever had about an hour to rush off a sketch, get back down to the office and help set up the copy. "Dreadful Death in Clapham." "Shocking Murder in Wandsworth." "Part-time Prostitute Found in River." I would have been there when they fished poor Jacky out, had I not become a painter.

So, I took a leaf out of Michelangelo's book and went to study corpses. There's a morgue at Quiberon, and the doctor in charge has artistic pretensions and no-one to talk to. In exchange for a little scandalous conversation and a few paintings, he gave me free run of the place. Every corpse that came in, I looked at and studied. The more disfigured and decomposed the better. I became quite expert at depicting the effects of maggots, and of water, and of dog bites on tramps left too long in gutters; excellent in putting down in a few strokes of the pencil the beautiful red line that a knife across the throat will make. Of bones showing through green skin, of skulls beginning to surface through the face. The sort of detail even the most scurrilous of London magazines would not touch, let alone a patron of the arts.

But it still wasn't good enough, and d'you know why? Because they were dead. They had no character, no personality. Obviously not, you say, and I don't want to stress the obvious. But the only way you can depict the flight of character, of the soul, is if you have known the person in life. The man who sculpted Louis XII must have known him well. The absence of personality wells out of that statue like a great hole; you can know the man by what is no longer there.

I HOPE YOU NOTICE that I have radically altered my technique since you last saw me. I have done away with those vastly long brushes that used to be my stock in trade. A pity, in some ways, as they looked so good. I remember the photograph that went with the review of my first big show at the Fine Art Society in 1905. I was more proud of the photograph than the reviews, I think, good though they were.

Now there, I thought, *there* is a painter. And it was true. I was a handsome dog, and every inch the artist, standing so proud some three feet from the canvas, with that long thin brush extended before me. A bit like the conductor of an orchestra, forcing my colours to take on the shape and shades I required. Big brush strokes, very Impressionist. But it was all thirty years too late, wasn't it? We were so proud of ourselves for challenging the establishment, bravely taking on the academicians, banishing the dusty and fusty, the conventional and the staid. But they were already dying on their feet anyway, those old codgers. We didn't really have to fight; our generation never has. Never will, either; if there is a war now—and people tell me there may be one day—it won't be us marching along, rifle in hand. We're too old already. Besides, we were merely imitators, importers of foreign ware into England, with no more originality than the people we so greatly despised. Less, perhaps; you would never have mistaken one of their pictures for a French one; our radicalism consisted of making ourselves copyists.

Ah, but it looked good for a while, no doubt about it, and it was the way to make a living, win a reputation. The English cannot take too much novelty; thirty-year-old fashions are quite radical enough for them. Not a criticism; it's comfortable and safe, but even then I think I was aware that our excitement and fervour were not quite genuine. There was always something of the amateur theatricals about us. So I went back to the beginning when I came here. I'd been a good enough painter, but not an entirely honest one, so I started again. Out went those long-handled brushes, in came perfectly ordinary ones, the sort you can get at any supplier's. Change that, and you change everything. The movement of the brush on the canvas, how much paint you pick up, how you mix it. I am more precise, more considered and meticulous now. And I am more interested in what I am painting.

A big change. My inability to remember the name of that woman I so horribly insulted was no accident. I can scarcely remember any of my sitters; could hardly remember them then. I didn't know them when they came into my studio for the first time, and knew them scarcely any better when they left clutching their finished portrait. I painted what I thought they looked like, how the light reflected off their clothes and skin, the interplay of colours around them. Character and personality played second fiddle to technique. And that was not good enough. Reynolds knew that, and said so. Rembrandt knew it so well he couldn't even be bothered to mention it. He no doubt wanted to paint the soul, Reynolds wanted a psychological study, but it was the same thing they were after, really. What lies beneath; the skull beneath the skin, and the soul within the skull—or wherever it may be found.

And I was putting down a lazy, superficial glance, thinking that because it was *my* glance, put down in the latest French style, it was enough. All I was saying was: Look at me! Aren't I clever? A very poor thing, that. I have concluded that unless you are humble before your subject, you are no good. And it doesn't matter whether your subject is the King-Emperor of Britain and the Indies, or a cheap model, or a bowl of fruit.

You see the link, no doubt? Of course you do, you got there way before me; you were always cleverer than me. I am trying to justify why it is that most Sundays you will find me on my knees in the local church. I am trying to become a better painter, my friend, because if the Almighty doesn't make me feel humble, the pasty face of William Nasmyth smirking before me in my best chair is hardly likely to do so either. I am trying to paint you, inside and out, and that is why I find it all so difficult. You are a hard one to fathom, always have been, because you have always been a bit of a charlatan.

There! That's what I mean! Most people would look displeased at that, a little concerned at least. I have never met anyone, however despicable, who does not believe that they are fundamentally decent. It is part of the human condition.

Nothing to be done about it. We need to feel as though we are doing our best. We need to justify our ways, to ourselves even if to no-one else. But you are different. You smile at the accusation. Not in a dismissive way, either, as if to say, foolish man, you cannot touch me so easily. No; with you there is the slightest, smallest nod. Of agreement. Of course I am a charlatan, that little inclination of your head says. That is my profession. We live in an age when appearance is all, and I am the master of it. I am a purveyor of the new upon the public, the intermediary. I persuade people to love what they hate, buy what they do not want, despise what they love, and that can only be done with the techniques of the circus ringmaster. But I am honest, nonetheless, and tell the truth. In that lies my integrity: I am a fraud with a purpose.

"What do all men desire, except fame?" That was the question you put to me one night in a pub in Chelsea. We were a little drunk, I recall, so I didn't reply; I knew you were going to answer for me anyway. I liked those evenings; to talk of such things, surrounded by the boatmen drinking away their wages, the porters and the grocers getting louder and louder as the publican pocketed their children's food for the next week. It still meant a lot to me, though I was beginning to touch my emancipation by then. Your words were no longer received uncritically, and I was coming to see myself as your equal in stature. Is that not what a good teacher does, after all, stands and watches his pupils grow through, then outgrow, his tutelage? But then I realised you did not want me to grow. Just as much as I needed you to teach me, you needed my worship and naïveté and were not prepared to do without. I often wonder what it must be like to be a father, to see your child no longer childish, losing that automatic tendency to adore. Does it come in a moment, or gradually? Is it a peaceful or a violent process? Is that why artists behave like children, needing to humiliate and denigrate their elders in order to feel sure of themselves?

I suppose I will never find out. I will not see forty-five again, and it is too late; children are a form of creation that I will not experience. My decline is imminent; already I feel my bones ache when I get out of bed, feel tired at the end of the day, have trouble seeing things as well as I once did. It is the great curse of the portraitist, to be so aware of one's own decline. I have spent years looking at people's faces and bodies, know which muscles need to sag to produce that look of diminution in the elderly. I see a face and can trace the lines creeping across the cheeks and forehead, the way the eyes sink and lose their lustre. I have to see my fate every time I look in a mirror. I can foresee the future. It was no shock to me when you arrived. I knew exactly what you would look like; knew the precise shade of grey that flicks your hair, how far the hairline had receded, what difference it would make when more of that high forehead was revealed. Nothing bad, by the way; it adds to the air of intellectuality. I also knew in advance that your hands have become more bony, so that the impression of claws is accentuated. The fates have reserved corpulence for my decrepitude; you are awarded an ever more skeletal appearance, the skin of the neck beginning to drag down in lines like a lace curtain. I also knew that age would not have lessened that angularity that makes you seem uncomfortable and ill at ease. It has made it worse, in fact; you now seem to have no patience for anyone in the world. If you get older, that will get more pronounced. You can look forward to no physical ease; your body will not permit it. The inevitable beckons already; time is short.

I still enjoyed your company, long after we came back to London. I looked forward to our evenings, when you would, as much as possible, stop being the critic, and I would stop being—whatever I was trying to be at the time. It all ended when you married, alas; then you became domestic and proper, and went to clubs instead of taverns, and dinner parties instead of whelk stands. You lost the last slither of your integrity in Mayfair, and learned to hide the earnest intensity that had always redeemed you. Slowly you said less that was good about people, more that was bad. Didn't you miss it, though? On those night-time voyages we were adventurers in the dark lands of London, seeing subjects for paintings down dingy alleys, or huddled in doorways. We thought of ever more exotic places to meet: a tea shop in Islington; a chophouse at Billingsgate; a tavern in Wapping; a dance hall on a Saturday night in Shoreditch where we would watch the clerks and the cleaners, the cooks and the shop girls as they forgot their cares for a few inexpensive hours. There was something of magic in those places for me, something you do not get at the Athenaeum. A recklessness, and an energy, and a desperation. The very stuff of paintings, I think, if only a means can be found of persuading people to buy it.

And there was that pub in Chelsea, the only place we went more than once. Poorly lit, with terrible food and the air so heavy with tobacco smoke you could scarcely see the person across the table from you. So thick that a river fog outside was easier to see through. Stiflingly hot from so many bodies crammed in, and smelling dreadful from the sweat and beer, cheap food and pipes. But I remember looking at it, and suddenly saw the place come alive; not tobacco brown, but brilliant colours—the red of a neck scarf, the orange of an Irishman's hair, the purple of a whore's dress. The gold of the landlord's cherished watch-chain, the ambers and browns and whites of the bottles on the shelves. And all those bodies, contorted and hustled together like a Renaissance battle scene. This is where the great tragedies and comedies of the modern world are played out. Not on an imagined medieval battlefield. And not in the South Seas, nor yet in Paris. There.

But do you remember how it all faded as we settled in? I do; I remember those conversations as though we were in an empty room, with no difficulty hearing or being heard, with no one bumping into us, as we sat and talked and drank and laughed, with you leaning over the table, your eyes blazing with the fire that came over you when you were fully engaged with an idea. You did not yet argue for pleasure, or merely to win. The truth still mattered to you.

"What do all men desire, except fame?" I did look around then, and you took the point. Did these people desire fame?

"Of course they do, in their little way," you said. "Fame in their limited universe; the fame of being a good drunk, a generous fellow, one amongst everyone else. They wish their reputation to extend as far as their eyes can see. But as that is not too far from the end of their noses, then that is what they aim at. Artists see farther, so their ambitions are greater. They want the world to bow down before them, not just in this generation, but in the generations to come.

"But how to do it? Eh? Do you think that merit alone can achieve it? Do you think Michelangelo without Pope Julius, Turner without Ruskin, Manet without Baudelaire, would be so famous? Do you think merely painting good pictures is enough? You are a fool if you do."

I suggested, I think, that poor Duncan, who you were then avidly promoting, could hardly be compared with Michelangelo.

"You are being obtuse," you said. "Duncan transfers my ideas into physical form. I am not a painter, never was, never will be. I see the pictures I want in my mind, but cannot paint them. Duncan will do it for me. The time of the patron is long gone. It is not the people who buy paintings who matter, not even the artist who paints them. This is the age of the critic, of the thinker on art. The man who can say what art means, what it should be."

I suggested that perhaps the public could make up its own mind. Not seriously, of course.

A snort of derision. "The public wants cheap filth. Over-painted nudes and pretty landscapes. We live in an unprece-dented age, my friend. For the first time in history one group of people has the money, and another has the discernment.

Admit it. You know it every day. How do you earn your money? You paint one thing to survive, and another to feel honest."

You swept your arms around at the room, which had lost its colour and had become tobacco brown once more. "Look at these people! Hopeless. But at least they are poor. They are unlikely to put their hideous taste into practice, and besides, their money is not worth having, they have so little of it. All those people who dine at the Ritz are something else, more dangerous. They must be persuaded to buy something they do not like. And that is my job. Don't look so disapproving. Without me, you'll be painting big pink portraits of big pink women, of little girls on swings, for the rest of your life."

This is what I am putting down now, if you must know; just before the light changes and I will have to stop for the day. I hope I can catch it, and turn it into light and shade, greens and blues. It is a darkness, your ambition, a shadow on your face, and I fear I will not get it just right. I will hint at it merely, and develop the theme later. Because it is not all there is. You believed in your ideas, after all, and merely used doubtful means to promote them. The magnificence of your arrogance, the exuberance of your daring, your sincerity and your cynicism, all these must find their place, translated into reality through the mixture of shadow and light, of colour and texture.

No theories here, you see. I am done with them, never believed in them anyway, really. We went our separate ways, after all. As you pointed out, I did not have enough money to paint things no-one would buy. The Banker's Wife must be made to look like a pillar of society; only then will you get a banking price for your work. I lived a double life, running between drawing rooms and the dingy meetings of your art clubs, trying to reconcile the two, and failing, as you knew I must.

A man must eat, my friend! A man must eat. You could disdain those wealthy bankers because you were as rich as one, thanks to your wife. But I could not; I could either have success in the world or esteem from you. You urged me to have both, but it was another piece of your trickery. Because it could not be done.

And you don't know the half of it. Do you want a confession? I turned faker too, in those days. You faked opinions on paintings; I faked the paintings themselves. People would not pay for my work, so I would produce things they would pay for. What was more, I duped you, once.

Ah! At last, I have got through those finely hewn defensive walls of yours. Thank heavens. It was my last throw. If that hadn't worked, I would have had to resign myself to failure. You see, you are vulnerable as well. A little flicker, a momentary uncertainty; that was all I needed from you.

That's enough. I'm not going to do any more today. So you have an afternoon free to vegetate, read, go for walks, write letters. Whatever you do with yourself. You may have noticed it is getting cooler these days as autumn approaches. The seasons change fast here. Better enjoy the sun while it lasts. Another day or so and the atmosphere will become violent.

SO MUCH FOR my prediction! A fine morning, again, although I detect the first touch of cold in the wind, which has switched to the northwest. Believe me; I know what I am talking about. You would not notice it, I imagine; you have to live here for a long time before you become sensitive to the minuscule changes in the weather. It's a certain freshness just after dawn, the lightness of the wind, the sound of the sea that makes the difference and lets you know we are on the slide down into another winter. We really will have a storm in a day or so; I hope so, I want you to see one. The moods of the weather delight me; until I came here I never realised how much I hated the English winter. You become the weather you live in—I know, it's a cliché, but I never realised quite how true it was. The drabness of the English climate produces drab people, wrapped up, desperate to keep the outside at bay. They wear an emotional overcoat throughout their lives and scowl upwards, wondering whether it is going to rain again. Quite right, too; it is. But it is not uplifting, to be enclosed by a feeling that if it isn't raining now, it will be tomorrow. And we Scots . . . how can anyone understand colour when half the year it is only light six hours a day? You can crave it, of course, stand in front of a Claude Lorrain and wonder whether such blues truly exist in nature, dream of being in a place where the evening sun lights up poplar trees with such contrast and intensity. But that is not the same as understanding it, sinking into that brilliance and losing your fear of it. Such colours will always be foreign.

Here it is different, although I'm not sure why. We are only off the coast of Brittany, after all, not in the tropics or North Africa. But the weather gods are more direct here, unlike in England where they insinuate that it is summer so quietly that you could easily miss it, or ooze their way into winter so slowly you scarcely notice the change. Here they announce it with a trumpet blast, with tempests and heatwaves, cloudless blue skies or rainstorms that can batter you onto your knees, with howling winds or air so still and quiet you can hear a woman talking half a mile away.

Can I tell you my earliest memory? You are being my confessor, after all, after a fashion. I know you do not want to be one, but you have no choice. You are my prisoner, trapped by your bizarre desire for a portrait by my hand. And as I said, I have been practising confession of late, and find it pleasing. Do you know, I was talking to my doctor a year ago in Quiberon—I had gone for another potion to help me sleep, although few have had much effect except laudanum, which gives me such a headache I prefer not to use it—and he told me about this man in Vienna who has revived the confessional and turned it into medicine. He is a little cut off, my poor doctor, a small-town provincial physician on the fringes of civilisation, so he subscribes to all the latest journals and societies. Anyway, this Austrian Jew has come up with this idea which rather struck my medical friend. You go along with some ailment, talk for months and—poof!—you feel better. And that's it, apart from paying over the money. You look sceptical; I am not. Of course it works, I am merely astonished that people will pay for it. My confession to you is making me feel better, as well, and do not think I am talking for no purpose. I have a very real purpose; I am confessing my sins in advance, before I have committed them. Explaining my painting to you, so you will understand it. See why I have chosen to do it in this way, rather than any other.

So my earliest memory was of being beaten by my mother. I must have been about four, I suppose, maybe less. It was winter, and cold, and night-time. I needed to go to the toilet, but my mother had forgotten the nightstand and I couldn't bear the long walk down to the privy at the end of our little garden, shivering with cold, and the wind cutting through my thin dressing gown. So I stood by the door and hesitated. Too long, and I peed in my pyjamas and it ran down my leg and over my foot and all over the floor which she had just finished washing down. I knew I'd get into trouble, and started to cry. I was right. My mother came down and beat me for it. Then she made me go down on my knees, and pray God for His forgiveness.

I know why, of course. There was never enough money or food or clothes, and she was exhausted, always near her wits' end. She worked, cooked, cleaned, mended, made do on far too little. Kept up appearances—can you even guess how onerous, how inviolable that need is in a small Scottish town? That was most of it. The rest was Scottish; the need to punish and the hatred of failing. All things, all infractions must be punished, however unwilled they were. Remember it; punishment is in my soul. I have travelled far in many ways but I have long since accepted that I can't escape. I am not complete without punishment, meting it out and being punished in turn. Life, like a good painting, needs balance, a harmonious arrangement to avoid being chaotic, a mess, a failure.

But it was at that moment, at the age of four, that I decided I would leave—which was precocious of me, you must admit. I swore that sooner or later I'd escape and never go back. Not to that home, that meanness, that littleness. That washing-on-a-Monday, watch-what-the-neighbours-think life, the castor-oil and prayer upbringing. Everything I have done has been propelled by that; this is what the priest says, as he tries to inculcate the love of Mary into me. He may be right, though I do not think things are so very different on this island. Besides, I will ever prefer God the avenger, the wrathful, the punisher. But I succeeded; I escaped.

Did you ever wonder how it was that a poor boy like myself, earning only five shillings a week in Glasgow, then a princely seven shillings a week in London, managed to make his way to Paris and live there without any work? Probably not; where money comes from has never been a concern of yours; it has always been there. It is no more surprising to you than water coming out of a tap. But I had to sell my soul for it.

I am not joking. I cannot even claim that it was on impulse, or something that I truly regretted. I stole the money from my mother. Her life savings, all she had for her old age after my father died. You notice I do not say borrowed, or took. I am not trying to hide anything. Stole. It was my only chance, my only hope of survival. It was her or me. When I decided I had to go to Paris, I made the long journey home, went to the little package she kept hidden under the bed, and took it all. She knew it was me, of course, but never said a word. It was her punishment for having brought me into the world. She knew it, and so did I; I was an agent of chastisement only. I think I did tell myself that I would give it all back, with interest, when my career prospered. But I never returned a single penny. She died before I had anything to give back, but I am not sure I would ever have done so. I didn't want to. She had to live out the rest of her life knowing she had a worthless, greedy, cruel son, and her pride and dignity meant she could not even tell anyone. It made it certain I could not go back there, ever. The guilt was like the walls of a fortress, forever keeping me out of Scotland, barring my way back to where I came from. And when she died, I did go back. But not to her funeral. She was buried alone, and I don't even know where. She was a wicked woman, harsh and punishing, who used her own sufferings as a weapon against her child and her husband. She deserved no pity, and got none from me.

Now, to work. I have finished sketching, had enough experimenting with your fine features. I tried all sorts of angles and poses in my head, and have settled on the one that was in my mind from the very beginning. The characteristic one you have of sitting in a chair with one shoulder slightly forward, and your head fractionally turned towards it. It gives you a sense of being about to move all the time, of energy. Quite undeserved, I think, as you are one of the laziest people I have ever known. Your energy is not physical at all; it is a fine case of the body reflecting the mind, creating an illusion which has nothing to do with the pills for the heart, weak arms and your tendency to puff and wheeze your way up stairs. It is an example of the superiority of the will over reality; I could beat the hell out of you, pick you up and carry you halfway across the island even against your will. Most people could; but I suspect the idea has never crossed anyone's mind since you were at school—where I imagine you were bullied, as children do not appreciate the power of the intellect. A further problem to be solved, of course— for the painting must convey the intellect through the physical—how to communicate the strength of one and the weakness of the other at the same time?

I'm not asking your advice; merely posing the question. It would be a fatal error to ask any sitter how they wished to be portrayed. People cannot tell the truth about themselves, for they do not know it. What do you think the balance should be between painter and subject, in any case? I know your answer without even asking, really. The subject is merely the means by which the painter expresses himself. The painter is merely the means through which the critic's ideas take form. It is a route that runs to perdition, you know; it will cut the artist off from everything but his own ego, sooner or later, and he will have an eye for nothing but what the *Morning Chronicle* says of him.

Enough of this. You are looking weary, and it gives you a faintly undignified expression. I cannot stand it. I keep seeing that rather bony bottom of yours sliding uncomfortably across my chair, and the vision is beginning to hinder my work. So I suppose I had better continue with my confession and tell you when I duped you. I could see by the look on your face when you came in that you wanted to know. Indeed, I had a fond, and slightly malevolent, pleasure in thinking about you going to sleep last night, tossing and turning in your uncomfortable, flea-ridden bed, wondering which of the tens of thousands of pictures you have viewed in your life showed you up to be a fool. Not a great one, certainly, but a small one; that, for you, is the worst of all, is it not? The idea that someone out there is laughing at you. And how many other people have been told? Is it common knowledge? Did you go into parties and hear someone snigger, all those years ago? Is that what they were laughing at?

Relax, I do not have that much malevolence in me; you should know that by now. I am not above a practical joke, I can be cruel, but am only rarely mean. Only on special occasions. My lips were sealed; it was a private pleasure, and all the more enjoyable for that. Besides, the whole business was unimportant in comparison to the result of it.

Shall I give you a hint? No; don't try to guess, it will only make it worse if you panic and decide that genuine masterworks were by my hand. It was a Gauguin. That painting which occupied a small place in your smoking room before you sold it to that American woman. I felt like telling you then, because you got a respectable sum for it and I felt I should have had a share. It's not as if I sold it as a Gauguin, after all. My conscience is clear. In a museum now? Good heavens, how gratifying! I must write to them before I die, or better still, I will leave a note in my papers so that if someone ever writes a biography of me, the information will come out then.

I painted it for purely innocent reasons, I assure you, and

had no intention of selling it to anyone. But do you remember when news of this man first came to us? How some shrugged and dismissed him, while you became convinced that he was the greatest thing since—the last greatest thing? I was intrigued, and went along to that dealer who had some of his pictures. I studied them hard, you know; sketched them, examined them meticulously, tried to figure them out. And got nowhere; baffled completely. So I decided to paint one, to see if that could give me any insight.

It did me no good. Whatever merit he possesses does not lie in his skill; he is not a skilled painter, speaking from a technical viewpoint, and I already found my simplicity in the East End; I saw no need to rush to the other side of the world for it. Besides, they seemed rather fraudulent to me, and I felt rather sorry for those poor native women splodged onto his canvas. They were just puppets, nothing more; no individuality or existence of their own. He was using them, not looking at them. He travelled right across the world and still could see only himself. At least colonialists provide sewage and a railway line to those they exploit. He took and gave nothing in return whatsoever. Nonetheless, a Gauguin I painted, and rather a good one, it seems, as it fooled not only you but everyone else as well.

I was going to paint over it when I'd finished, but Anderson came to visit. This was shortly after he had abandoned painting and gone into art dealing. "Get between the painter and his public, my boy." That was his business, and he proceeded to squeeze his svelte little body into just that position; taking more, giving less. The recipe for brilliance as a dealer. You, I recall, were properly sneering at his decision, and were highly critical of the consummation of his marriage to Mammon, although I never really saw that there was so great a difference between him and you.

You hurt him, you know; and very badly. Under that don't-give-a-damn façade there beat the heart of a sensitive soul. He really wanted to be a painter—far more than you could ever understand. He had set his heart on it when he was eight, so he once told me. Can you imagine his anguish, poor man? To have everything necessary except true ability? His eye was exceptional, his taste exquisite, his sense of colour remarkable, his feeling for proportion and structure was near perfect. Technically he was highly accomplished. He worked hard. But try as he might, he couldn't put it all together, couldn't harness those skills into a harmonious whole. So, rather than be a bad painter, permanently disappointing himself, he became a dealer instead.

You were the one who forced him to give up, you know.

That winter when he took a studio near the Tottenham Court Road and went underground, living like a hermit, doing nothing but work all the daylight hours God sent. By day he painted, the rest of the time he sketched and drew. He became obsessed; I could see it on his face on the rare occasions I bumped into him. The darkness of too little sleep, the slightly hunched air of one trying to defy the world but knowing he is taking a gamble that might well not come off. A man trying to ignore what he already knows in his heart.

He was painting for his life, working away to try and tip over that edge into—what? Not competence or expertise; he had those already. He wanted to be good, and he thought he was getting there. He persuaded himself this burst of work was inspiration, that finally he had let loose whatever it was that proved so difficult.

Eventually he finished. About a dozen paintings, one of which he planned to submit to the next New English exhibition. But he was living in his mind, and knew that sooner or later these works would have to be shown to others. So he invited us to a small dinner. Just you and me; the people he trusted. You must remember it! I know you do; you'd be lying to deny it. I recall every second. It was one of the most distressing evenings of my life.

His tension, his agitation were terrible. I could understand why he was nervous of you; you had already established yourself as the great arbiter of the modern and the worthy, and if he was frightened of me it was only by association. I have never been a severe critic of others. He did his best to be hospitable, dropping things on the floor, spilling wine on the table; I could hardly bear it. Poor man! I thought he was prolonging the social niceties because of gaucheness; but I was wrong. Miserable as it was, he wanted it to last as long as possible. I think that in his heart he knew already they were the last few moments when he would be able to think of himself as a painter.

Eventually the moment came. "Oh yes, I have been working. Quite a lot, in fact. Pleased with my efforts. Think they'll be more than good enough." The staccato phrases, delivered with a fake drawl of self-confidence, only showed how on edge he was. "Want to see them? Oh, very well then, if you must . . ."

Then it began. One by one, the pictures brought out; one by one, put on the easel; one by one, a grunt or sniff from you, and the silence of increasing despondency from me. Surely you remember them? They weren't that bad. They really weren't. They were competent, even charming. But mechanical and lifeless—frozen people, dead landscapes,

pointless interiors with no shape or form. How could he not
see? How could he not do better?

And when he had finished, you started. Picture by picture.
Perhaps you began in the spirit of constructive criticism, I
don't know. But as you worked your way through each canvas, the joy of the hunt came upon you. The pitilessness of it
was terrible. Every fault, every weakness you spotted and
pointed out; each painting was dismantled, colour by colour,
line by line, form by form. Nothing escaped you: it was a
tour de force, a brilliant piece of sustained, improvised destruction. And throughout it all, poor Anderson had to sit
there, politely, respectfully, not able to show on his face how
you were torturing him as you ground his dreams to dust.
He hoped, no doubt, that you would clap your hands and ac-
claim each one as a masterpiece. At the very least, he hoped
for dishonesty on your part; polite praise and a promise to
put in a word with some hanging committee, to find a place
on their walls for one picture, to give him a chance.

But dishonesty was not in your character—not then, at
any rate. That would have been a betrayal of something
more important than friendship, of mere human relations.
Anderson was no good. That was all that concerned you.
It was his job to face up to it. Your job to make him do so.
You were cruel in the name of art, vicious in its protection.

You left him a hollow man, for you took away his dreams and showed him what he really was. The critic as mirror: unflattering, harsh, but bitterly truthful.

I could not have done it. I would have taken the polite, dishonest, reassuring route. It would have led to the same place eventually, no doubt. Nor could I disagree with what you said; as ever, you were right, each fault was real, and you did not exaggerate. You were judicious in your devastation, calm in your violence.

But still, I did catch that flicker in your eye, something of the sort that I had seen once before. A hidden pleasure, a satisfaction. Power controls the artist. You were laying claim to that power, flexing your muscles. You decided who was or was not to be counted in the ranks. And you expelled Anderson.

I know; you didn't realise how badly you hurt him, but why you look so concerned now I don't understand. It wouldn't have made any difference. Besides, you never asked, and Anderson was expert at hiding his sadness. What are schools for, after all? And he had been to a good one which had taught him how to present the right face to the world. So, to you, who did not trouble to look below the surface, he was more interested in money than painting. Nonsense. He longed to starve in a garret, poor man. Desired nothing better than to be shunned by the public, scorned by the galleries. If only he could please himself, he would have been more than happy. But he could not please himself, and you explained why not.

Were I meaner than I am, I could make much of this in my portrait, you know. Is not a critic someone who is meant to see below the surface? Can you be a judge of art but know nothing of the people who produce it? If you cannot under-stand your fellow man, can you understand what he pro-duces? Is this your weakness, that no matter how skillful your judgements, you never see the humanity which must lie un-derneath it? Or might I take the other view and think that perhaps you did see, and in your comments you were delib-erately turning the knife in the wound, adding ridicule to the sense of failure he already felt in abundance?

Either way, you made a quiet enemy that evening. So when he came to visit me and saw my Gauguin, the thought occurred to him. A little joke, we told ourselves, but both of us knew it was more than that. We were going to expose you. You had just come out with that article on the primitive folk of the South Seas, where you praised the clarity of vi-sion that could not be achieved in England. And so on, and so on. Magisterial, informed, influential, nonsense. There was always a side of you which could tip slightly into windbaggery, and this was one of those occasions. So next time you visited Anderson's gallery, he got his assistant to whisper that you should go into his office, and look at the picture leaning against the wall.

"The boss doesn't like it," he was told to say. "What do you think?"

Oh! the pleasure we had—don't squirm so in your seat; you'll ruin the pose—as we used your money to pay for our celebratory meal. We went to the Café Royal, far beyond my normal range at the time. I remember the food being delicious, far more so than it could actually have been. Fish soup, roast lamb, followed by a crème brûlée of such perfection that it was a work of art itself, equal to the greatest productions of the old masters. It was the moment that made it taste so good. And do you know what happened, as we were toasting you for your generosity? Evelyn came in, with Sickert. I felt a pang of jealousy when I saw them together; it was the only brown shade on an otherwise gaily tinted evening. Sickert was at the height of his powers, and irresistible to all he chose to attract—until he decided to unleash that strain of cruelty which always lay hidden inside him. I imagined Evelyn being drawn into his circle, becoming one of his admirers, slowly having her originality drained away as she was coerced by his personality into producing second-rate imitations of his style. He was persuasive and forceful in ways even you could not manage. You bludgeon people with your intellect; he uses terror, fascination and that hypnotic charm which always worked best on women. Have you noticed how few men actually like him? And how few women have ever been drawn to you? That is an observation, not an insult, by the way; you and he divided the artistic world between you, one sex apiece. A pity; a contest between you would have been something to watch.

He failed with Evelyn, though, and as completely as you did. She found his charm absurd, his blandishments all too easily resistible. He, in turn, found her to be cold, devoid of emotion, frigid. She was too locked in herself, would never amount to anything until she let go—by which he meant, I imagine, until she submitted to him. Well, maybe there was something to that; certainly her caution was her best defence, and must have been hard learned. She wanted an artistic liaison, and turned away without hesitation when it became clear he had something less subtle in mind. He should have asked me first; I could have saved him the price of a few expensive meals.

Anyway, in they came and joined us for the last course. Do you know, it was the most delicious dessert I have ever eaten? Every mouthful made the more sweet by the possibility that, once it was swallowed, one of us was going to say, "Do you know who's paying for this meal . . . ?" Then the story would be let loose from its cage, and we would see it take wing, and flutter around London, leaving gales of laughter every time its shadow fell on the ground. But we didn't; that was the real joy. We exchanged many glances of complicity, came close to choking, on occasion, but we hugged it to us. You were *our* prey, not anyone else's. We did not need our triumph to become a public one.

And, yes, perhaps there was a little fear as well. I remember all too well how much you hate being talked about. I remember what you did to take your revenge on poor Rothenstein when some harmless comment he made about you came to your ears. You isolated him, humiliated him. Never let up; more than a decade later you went out of your way to exclude him from your exhibition. You forbade me, and anyone else close to you, to see him, talk to him, have anything to do with him. We were a little group before you arrived to reorganise us, we English speakers in Paris, companionable, trusting, easygoing. We weren't close, but naturally gravitated towards each other, learnt from each other, helped each other out.

We split into friends of Rothenstein and friends of yours, those who thought Evelyn was pleasant enough and those who delighted in making fun of her. Those who liked one painter, preferred another, this school or that school. You made sure little preferences became matters of principle important enough to cause bad feeling and rancour. Was Rodin a better sculptor than Bernini? David better than Ingres? Pissarro or Monet? It didn't matter which; I heard you argue on both sides. Divide and rule, the first principle of the despot.

Even I said you were being ridiculous, but always I treasured those walks, the conversations along the Seine or in the parks. I didn't want to risk too much, lest I lose them. My protests were muted.

"Are you with me or not?" was your only response. "Whose side are you on?"

"Is it a question of sides?"

"Yes. A few friends, the rest enemies. That's the way the world is. If you don't destroy them, they'll destroy you. You'll learn that eventually."

Then you went on a tirade about all those people—most of the world—you did not trust. It was a side of you I had never seen before; until then I had only seen the kindness, the generosity, the warmth. But all that was reserved for your loyalists; the punishment meted out to others showed something very different. Where did it all come from? Where did you learn to think that the world was a battle, with only winners and losers? Where did you learn the need to destroy your opponents before they destroyed you?

So my budding disloyalties remained hidden. You were my friend, after all, and I believe you should forgive friends their failings. It made me begin to think, though. I am not generally a nasty person, as I hope you will agree. And yet, underneath the surface of that little piece of cleverness over the Gauguin there was something decidedly unpleasant. I would not have enjoyed it so much had the painting been foisted on anyone else, however great their reputation, however skilled their judgement. It was because it was *you* that I so enjoyed my triumph. It took some considerable time before I figured out why doing that to a friend, my best friend, made me feel so good.

It is taking shape nicely now; I can do without you for the rest of the day. I am no Whistler, I do not like to torture my sitters, drive them to an early grave with my demands on their patience. When I need you back I will send a message. I will work in your absence for a couple of days on the toning and the light, which I can manage just as well in an empty room. Better, in fact, as you won't distract me. I can enter into your soul through the canvas and the paint, and make sense of you the better if you are somewhere else. I must paint what you were, and what you will become as well. Having you here in person is a complete nuisance.

I THOUGHT I would find a loophole in the rule I set. I don't intend to let you see the picture I am doing now; not least because I know you will not leave until you see it. It is my best hope of keeping you here until the bitter end. Someone who hates not being in the know will never leave until he has seen something so personal as his own portrait. I am surprised you have managed to contain yourself so far. I half expected you to hurl yourself across the room and grab the canvas. I wouldn't, if I were you. I could push you away easily, and it would merely make me more secretive. You do not give your subjects an advance look at the reviews you write about them, do you? So you can't expect a glimpse of something that is not even half completed. But I suppose there can be no harm in showing you the one I began eight years ago. It's yours, after all; paid for but never delivered. I've often wondered if you were irritated by the way I took the money and never gave anything in return for it. You can't complain too much; you offered far below my normal price, and I said at the time you might have to wait for it to be finished. Many a client has waited longer, as you know.

Here it is; what do you think? No; don't answer. I don't care what you think. It is incomplete. Not as a picture; it is more than finished, not another brushstroke needed. But as a portrait it is rather limited. I almost burned it a few years back, but I've always been reluctant to go for that sort of grand and wasteful gesture.

An autocritique, then. It is a portrait of a friend, and that is its fatal weakness, one which I have finally solved not by reworking it or burning it, but by continuing it into this new one. Do you know that I remember every moment of painting it? Even looking at it now fills me with a strange melancholy. It was—what?—1906, July 10, a Saturday, one of the most glorious days in God's creation. You'd suggested painting it in Hampshire, as you were spending the summer there, and I was more eager than I thought to get out of London. So I took the train from Waterloo at eight in the morning, with all my bags and easels tucked around me. God was in his heaven that day. My exhibition at the Carfax gallery was a success, not least because of your review of it; the money and commissions were beginning to come in handsomely, the house in Holland Park was slowly moving from being a dream to something that might shortly turn into solid reality. I had travelled far from Glasgow, and was nearing what I thought was my destination.

We had made it, you and I. You first, of course, with your wealthy wife, the books and articles, your place advising those American bankers, your trusteeships of museums, all the rest of it. But I, with my gruff Scottish manners convincing sitters they had an authentic artist on their hands, was on my way too.

So what could be more comfortable than to spend a week with my old friend, basking in mutual self-congratulation? Life cannot get much better than that morning. There was nothing that was not perfect, from the cup of tea I drank in bed before I left home, to the glass of cold wine that awaited me at your house with the view over the downs to the sea. Even the train was all but empty; I had the compartment to myself, and sat smoking my pipe in a dreamy content.

But. The worm of discomfort was there. Will it last? What if it doesn't? I wasn't thinking of any of that, of course, but it was in me, nurturing itself and waiting for its chance. The various elements that would bring me here were already forming around me and in me. What was I, after all? A painter, on the cusp of becoming successful, with two careers which I juggled incessantly. The portraitist and the other. The commanding figure with the long brushes, photographed for fashionable magazines, and the man who would spend his time sketching old dockers, poor refugees, tired shop girls, young men getting drunk in pubs and collapsing in the mud outside. Dreaming of the hopeless and the ill and the dead. They were increasingly my obsession, although I never showed them in public. They were dark pictures, unsellable. But that was not the reason I hid them. They were not very good and I knew it. It wasn't misplaced self-doubt, either. There was still too much of the magazine illustrator about me. I painted with passion and energy, and the results were mediocre, condescending, and full of contempt for the subjects. And not the sort of thing anyone would want in their drawing room.

So I painted my society portraits, and went to more and more fashionable parties and knew more and more interesting people, and dreamed of Holland Park. How tempting, how glittering it all was! And how easy this success is, as well. All you have to do is give people what they want, reflect themselves back into their own eyes, and they will fall over to crush money into your outstretched hand. I was becoming a businessman, and began thinking like one. I wanted particular commissions because of the exposure they would give me, the contacts I would make, not because they were interesting people with complex personalities or difficult faces.

I came to your house and began to paint you in your study. This picture, the critic as a young man, which I am now complementing with the critic in comfortable middle age. It intimidated me, that place. Those books, those precious objects of such variety. The Chinese porcelain, the wall hangings, the sculptures. The careless profusion of learning, the effortless ease of position. It was as natural to you as breathing, and you used it to bend others to your will. Don't pretend you didn't. And that had its effect on the portrait I painted as well. You imposed yourself on me; it was in every brush stroke. I painted not what I saw but how you wished to be seen.

Did you notice how I became more ill-humoured as the days wore on? You could scarcely have failed to. I behaved abominably, even by my own fairly tolerant standards. I played the artist, but badly, and without humour or grace. I was not like Augustus John, who can charm a woman as he seduces her daughter, amuse a man as he steals from his drinks cabinet. Nor did I want to; the more I stayed, the more I wanted to offend. And succeeded brilliantly, I think. Even I was surprised at my rudeness, my sneering remarks, because they were not normal for me. I am a well-mannered, polite little Scottish boy at heart, wanting to be well thought of by his betters. Did I really stay in bed until noon every day? Reduce your maid to tears with my ill-natured complaints? Say your daughter had better be clever because she'd never be pretty? I'm sure they were not all improvements I added on to the memory later. I was hoping you would throw me out, tell me you never wished to see me again. That you would let me free of your grasp.

But you do not let go of people so easily. You saw all too clearly what I was doing, better than I did. A look of long-suffering pain in your eyes, a smile of indulgence. A sugges-tion that perhaps I should spend the afternoon on my own. That was all I got in response. Because you knew I would not leave without your permission, just as you will not leave now without mine.

In truth, I should thank you, though. That trip to Hamp-shire brought my worries to the surface, set me on the road to France and the embrace of God in his most Catholic vari-ety. Because I realised, as I unpacked my paints and brushes, and got myself ready, that I was doing your bidding. You don't remember the moment, I am sure. I chose the position I wanted, and in my mind's eye I knew how I wanted you to sit. A stark portrait, it would be, head and shoulders, with nothing else to attract the eye. A bit Titian-like, I thought, the background so dark that it would be almost black, just a faint hint of a bookcase.

And what did I begin painting? The sunlight. I wanted to please you. No bad thing in a portraitist, of course, but the skill lies in making your own vision pleasing. I tried, many times over, to force myself into painting what I had imagined as I travelled down, but every time, the desire to please over-whelmed my instincts. And then I realised the truth: I was merely a hired hand, no different from the fat old woman you employed as a cook or the skinny little consumptive who served as your maid. They, at least, were under no illusions about their position, whereas I had persuaded myself that all these society women and gentlemen farmers who were fast becoming my stock in trade were something other than my masters. That I was their superior and your equal.

Not that I minded the clients so much; with them the re-lations were clear. They wanted a portrait making them-selves looking grander, more respectable, more human than they were, and were prepared to pay for it. I obliged; and as I was able to turn flattery into art—decent art as well; I never became a hack—they were happy to pay more than usual.

That was why I was a success, and in truth I am not ashamed of it. I did much good work; the problem was that it was not the work I wanted to do.

No; the problem was not my clients, who at least gave something in return for my subjection. They paid well and when the relationship came to an end—the money paid, the portrait hung—their power over me ended as well. The problem was you, who gave nothing and whose power never ended. The critic is a demanding god, who must be constantly appeased. You make your offering, then have to make it again, and again.

I lost my contentment during that trip to Hampshire. The sun had gone on the journey back to London; I felt every lurch of the train, the other people in the compartment irritated me. One stupid woman kept on trying to strike up a conversation, and I was extremely rude to her. I scowled at the ticket collector for no reason. Well, a very good reason, in fact.

THIS MORNING, I want to go for a walk. No; nothing subtle. It's not as if I want to get the colour into those pale aesthetic cheeks of yours, or make some point about bodily

exercise and spiritual insight, so I can translate it into a portrait in some masterful way. I merely feel like a walk, and I
am prepared to have your company. I walk fairly often, I'll
have you know. There is something always a little unsatisfac-
tory about it, mind. It is too enjoyable to walk here, except in
deepest winter. One does not suffer; there is no sense of triumph in the experience. I remember once going for a long
walk along Ardnamurchan shortly after I came back from
Paris. I went up to Scotland, just me and my sketch pad, to
draw anything and everything that took my fancy. I went
back to see if I could live in my homeland again; I really
wanted to, but knew the moment I got off the train it would
be impossible. Do you know there is no Scotsman who lives
in England who does not feel slightly guilty? Not about living in England, but about not wanting to go back. I have discovered that coming to France does not have the same effect.

Anyway, for three weeks I tramped over the land of my
forefathers. It was in my etching days, when all the world
wanted to be the Scottish Whistler, or the Irish Whistler,
or the Tunbridge Wells Whistler. Any place at all, as long
as critics like you made a comparison to Whistler. The
whole country, I believe, was awash with earnest young men
of middling talent, clutching little sheets of metal in their

hands, hunting for that perfect aspect, that moment in the doorway, so they could capture it and transmute it into copper, then gold, then fame.

It eluded me, of course; there is something about the Highlands that cannot be fixed down. Not by me, in any case. Look at the Highlands and you see suffering—if you can see at all. It is a ruined landscape, denuded of trees and people. There animals and men and forests have perished, and the weather reflects it. It is melancholy even when the sun shines. But not for everyone. You have to be tuned to the resonances to see the sadness, pick up the despair in the purple of the heather, the anguish in the wind as it whips up the waves on a loch surface. And if you are not, all you see is a landscape, and all you imagine is men in kilts with a bottle of whisky in one hand and a set of bagpipes in the other.

No one has ever picked up that misery in line; David Cameron picks up the spiritual side, but misses the human dimension. I tried; I came close, indeed, but not close enough and I didn't want them to be misunderstood. Can you imagine how it would have felt to have made pictures out of the landscape of human suffering and had them seen as pretty views of Highland scenes? That is what would have happened; I know, because I showed you some of my sketches once. You misunderstood them entirely because your eyes are forever turned towards the continent. The transcendental in your own backyard is of no interest to you. But you have never been to Scotland, never stood at the head of a glen with that wind nearly knocking you down, hearing it echo all around you, and listening to the generations who once lived there.

They talk, you know, the dead. Not in words, of course; I am not losing my sanity. They talk in the wind and the rain, in the way the light falls on ruined buildings and dilapidated stone walls. But you have to listen and want to hear what they have to say. And you do not; you are a creature of the present. The modern. Well, right enough. Savages and wild men they were. And now, it seems, rich savages, living off the fat of the land in America and Canada. Best thing that ever happened to them, leaving Scotland. What would that Carnegie have been, had he stayed in Scotland, eh? A poor weaver, all that boundless energy going into setting up illicit stills and drinking himself paralytic on a Friday night.

I can't hear the dead of this island. Not that they are not talking away; they are. Sometimes, late at night, I hear a sort of chattering in the wind as it rattles round the rooftops; occasionally a conversation almost starts up in the light shining through the puddles after a summer rain. But it never really gets going. We are on neighbourly terms, them and I; we nod to each other, smile occasionally as we pass, but have no desire to take our acquaintanceship further. I am a stranger here, after all, and they do not wish to burden me with their stories. And if they did, what could I say? I would listen politely, but could do little more.

So, eventually, I will have to leave. I will have to go back to Scotland, because if we do not have those conversations we wither a little every day. Oh, to be more portable! How convenient it must be to be Jewish, and carry your ancestors around with you, not needing lumps of dirty soil to strike up a conversation. They are reviled for it, but they are the fortunate ones, not us, who must pine away if we so much as move one country to the left or right.

Ardnamurchan? Oh. Yes. I went to recover from a broken heart. I had been rejected. Don't smile so; it is a bitter thing and to be avoided, as you always did avoid it. You never did love your wife, did you? I kept my own passion a secret. No-one wants their humiliations known, and I was refused when I went down on my knees and said my piece.

Evelyn, of course; I see I have surprised you. How inappropriate, you are thinking. What a bizarre choice. You would never be so careless; were not. You picked your wife with the same care you pick your clothes or your painters. Someone who will reflect well on you, help you along. Love does not come into it. But I loved Evelyn, I think, and that made all the difference.

You think? Don't you know? Surely it is not something you can be unsure about?

Well, yes. It is. If you have never felt the emotion before, and have had no practise. Love is not something that comes easily to people like me. It is too much bound up with sin. Love for God, that is simple. Love for your fellow man is also straightforward, if, generally speaking, quite unjustified. Love for a friend—quite easy although not without its complications. But love for a woman—ah, well now. That is the hardest, because it involves the carnal. Such feelings should surely be reserved for the low and the unworthy. To love a fine woman is to bring her down to the gutter.

Don't look at me like that! I'm not saying I approve, merely that this was how I was brought up. I am, after all, the only evidence that my parents ever even touched each other. When I grew up, when I was playing the painter, I bathed myself in all the lusts I could think of, to coat myself in sin and create a gulf between myself and my beginnings that was so wide I could never go back. But it was not with real pleasure; I did not truly enjoy sin, and that, of course, takes most of the point of it away. I sinned because I felt I ought to. Even fornication was turned into a duty. By running away from my origins, I found myself coming back to them, like an ant walking round the rim of a plate and ending up back where he started.

Evelyn was different, hence the proposal. I think I knew it the moment I first talked to her in Paris. We were alone in the atelier, and she had been strenuously ignored by everyone there. That wasn't unusual, I suppose; it was a sort of initiation rite, to test people out, see how tough they were. And she was a woman. At least we didn't riot and burn her canvasses, like the French students did when women were first let into the Beaux-Arts. Many a man was treated in the same way for a month or so. We were a group, and mistrusted outsiders. But enough was enough, and she clearly wasn't taking it very well, so I called over to her one evening, after everyone else had gone home.

"What do you think?" I asked. I'd been working hard all day on a painting, building it up from sketches I'd been making for the last month. I'd persuaded myself it was good. I was not yet vain, but I was growing rapidly in self-confidence. Besides, you had already seen it and paid fulsome compliments. I was letting her see it to give her a little treat. Show her what good painting was. I didn't want her opinion, and expected only her admiration and her thanks for including her, taking her seriously.

Evelyn came over and looked. Very seriously, with a frown on her face. But not for long. "Not very good," she said, eventually.

"Pardon?"

"It's not very good. Is it? It's too cluttered. What is it? A woman in a kitchen? She looks more as though she's finding her way through a junk shop." She paused, and thought some more. "Clean out the background, let the eye go to the woman herself. The pose is fine, but you're wasting it. Where's the centre? What's the point? If you want the viewer to figure it out, you've got to give them a little help. What are you trying to do? Show how clever you are? How much you're in charge of perspective and colour?"

"That's your opinion?"

"It is. And you will no doubt disregard it completely. But then, you shouldn't have asked."

And her eyes went back to the canvas, then flickered back to me, for a brief moment. There was laughter in them, even though her face was otherwise totally solemn. She knew full well she was being presumptuous considering I was both older and more experienced than she. She was testing me, seeing how I would react. Would I be pompous, take umbrage and start lecturing her about the fine qualities of my work? "No, no, you don't understand it. If you look . . ."

But that is not where my vanity lies. And the faint twinkle of amusement in her eyes touched me. I laughed myself. I wasn't completely sure she was right, although cramming too much in has always been a weakness of mine. But we signed a contract with that glance. The complicated relationship of fawning and flattering she had seen when I was with you was not her way. She would give neither. And I wanted neither from her. From that moment on I liked her but was also a little disconcerted. For she had challenged you with those remarks, and bit by bit I saw how empty your compliments could be. You were being lazy with me; you did not take me so seriously after all. She was right about the picture; you were not. You were fallible.

On the other hand, I rarely showed her any of my pictures again. Not the ones I cared about, anyway. I was too frightened of what she would see. A man can take only so much criticism. I never thought she might be equally wary of my opinion about her efforts.

Do you know what it's like to like someone, you who acknowledges no equal? Not to see all things in hierarchy, not to strain to be better, or more powerful, than the person you are with? Not to classify someone as friend or enemy, dependent or patron? Not to envy or be envied? It is friendship; I thought it might also be love. I still can't tell them apart.

I have had my passions and infatuations, although far fewer than my reputation might suggest, but there is enough of the Church of Scotland in me to have a suspicion of the fleshly thrall. Certainly I discovered that the magic always faded fast; no woman, however opulent, however seductive, interested me for very long. Not in the way that Evelyn did, and I was never attracted to her in that way at all. I think I wanted to know her, and the more my friendship with you faded and became bound by conditions and doubts, the more I craved her uncomplicated simplicity. I walked with her round London and Paris too; but it was a different experience. She didn't want to teach, nor did she lecture. When she looked at a statue or building, she did not wish to classify and pigeon-hole. There were none of the flat condemnations or soaring praise that you would deliver; she always tried to appreciate what the artist had been doing, however poor the result. She even found a good word for those pompous old goats from the Beaux-Arts. And above all, she took these walks because of companionship, nothing more. But there was always something in her which held back, which seemed afraid—I even thought seemed repelled—by my presence when I stood close to her. Yet she was so open at the same time. How could that be? It infuriated and frustrated me, and that, I decided, must be a symptom of love.

Coming to a decision took a long time. I delayed till we both came back to England, then some more until my career began to prosper a little, but eventually, in spring 1904, I made up my mind and proposed. Abruptly, and with little romantic style, I must say. I hadn't even seen much of her for some time when I went round to have my say. Flowers and gifts and all the sort of thing one should employ to create a special moment did not occur to me, which is just as well as it would have been wasted money. She turned me down flat; all I got was a look of shock and astonishment and, even worse, slight anger. Even the idea offended her. I could not see why, then. No-one else was going to make her an offer, and most women, so I had always believed, were at the very least flattered to be asked.

I suppose she was right; I hardly made a good case for myself, and at the time I had little to offer except a vast selfishness and a small income. I had never learned courtship, had never needed to; I thought that directness spoke for itself, but hadn't realised that the English like their ritual and distrust plain speaking as somehow mendacious. Everything has a hidden meaning, does it not? And the more direct the speech, the more carefully hidden the true meaning must be, the more effort must be expended to understand what is really being said. So much for my efforts at courtship, though, come to think of it, I have just summarised your philosophy as a sage of the modern. Your criticism is merely the sensibility of the English bourgeois applied to canvas. Nothing can be without explanation.

"I will never marry," she said, once the surprise had dissipated and she could speak again. At least she did not smile as she said it; that would have been too much. "I am not fitted for it. I do not desire children, and I believe I can look after my own needs, so I see little point in it. I can think of no man I like more than you," she went on, "and no man whose company I enjoy more. But that is hardly sufficient. No, Henry MacAlpine. Find someone else. I would never make you happy, and you would never make me content. I'm sure someone else will do a better job for you than I ever could."

And that was that. She discouraged any return to the subject, and even avoided me for some time, just in case I was minded to take up the matter again. So off I went to walk in the rain of the Highlands. My pride was hurt, of course, whose would not be? But I discovered that the occasional pangs of jealousy I felt whenever I saw her in the company of some man—a rare enough event—faded soon enough. It took some time before we resumed our old friendship, before she felt safe enough in my presence and was sure I was not about to go down on my knees again, but eventually calm was restored. I didn't know what she wanted, but soon enough I accepted that I was not it. And I easily persuaded myself that she would have been quite the wrong choice for me, as well. She was, after all, a very difficult person to be around. Moody, withdrawn, quixotic. No; it took only a short while to persuade myself I had been saved from a terrible mistake.

Don't think, by the way, that I didn't notice the look of scorn on your face as I was talking of my beloved homeland. Oh, so poetic about Scotland, and so far away from it! If it is so wonderful what am I doing on a little island off the coast of Brittany? If so patriotic, why head south instead of north? True enough; the most rapturous Scots are the nostalgic ones. Scotland stifles me; the landscape gives you a sense of freedom, the civilisation oppresses. I cannot paint there, because I am too aware of God's disapproval and of the impossibility of ever pleasing Him. Here I have at least persuaded myself He is a little more open to persuasion.

YOU SEE that my style has changed? Of course you have; you never miss anything. Along with the brushes, I have jettisoned the method. What were we taught? Line, line, line. And the immediacy of the impression; the two great irreconcilables that have destroyed a generation or more of English painters. There we were, slopping down great gobs of paint trying to fix something glimpsed for a moment then half forgotten. As Monet had shown us, so we did. Well and good; it produced a few pretty things, although personally there was always some little Calvinist inside me tutting away about French corruption. By all means, try and capture that brilliant flash of light on the lily pond; the play of autumn sun on the cathedral façade. But we never get much sun in Scotland, you know. Not much light, either. We have fifty-nine different shades of grey. We are a nation *en grisaille*, and can see all of God's creation in the difference between an overcast dawn and a threatening, squally morning. Even the green of the hills is grey, if you study it properly. The heather and the lochs, all on a grey ground. The sun itself is a grey sun. Grey is not an immediate colour. It makes no instant impression. You cannot paint it like that. You have to study grey for years—generations, I might say—before it will reveal its secrets. And then you have to paint deep, not on the surface. It would be like asking Tiepolo to paint his confections using the city councillors of Glasgow instead of the nobility of Venice. If you tried, the result would be laughable. Better not to try, and think of something else.

Or leave, of course. There are some Scots who have

reached that conclusion, abandoned the land of their birth and headed for the Mediterranean so they no longer have to use so much grey paint. I can imagine what they must say back in Dundee. "Och, mon, it's sae very garish. Will ye just will look at that, noo? Have ye everr seen a girrul with an orrrange face before? I wouldnae hae' that in ma hoose if ye paid me." I used to sneer at the Jute merchants of Dundee as well, all import ledgers and profit tallies, living in a world of penny counting and constraint. But they are right, after all. You have to make sense of what is around you, not dream of something so far away it is unattainable. You never do get girls with orange faces in Dundee; never see the sun refracted on the clear blue water.

So I have changed the style. Out with the brushes, out with the splodges. I want depth, not immediacy, so I have gone back to the methods taught me long ago and investigated others so long disused they have not been taught for generations. I build up the paint, layer by transparent layer. I have investigated glazes made of oil and egg yolk, different layers of transparency to add depth, to make the viewer work a little. Nothing now can be done or seen or understood instantly. Instead you have to look deep, as you do in a mist, slowly seeing what lies underneath the surface, making out the vaguest outline of—what? A hill, a skull, a hint of malice in an expression covered by the sheen of perfect manners.

All this takes time, of course. It used to be that I could belt out a portrait in little more than an afternoon; then I would have to make my poor sitter rest immobile for hours while I doodled away, to clock up the hours and justify my fee. Or I would send them away, and the canvas—perfectly finished—would gather dust in a corner for months. Now they really do take a long time; I have become uneconomic; the prices I would have to charge would be extravagant indeed to maintain any lifestyle above the primitive.

Money? Heavens, I have enough. It wouldn't see you through a weekend, I'm sure, but my ancestors gave me that frugality which was so much of their character. I tried to fight against it; almost succeeded for a long period, but I'm afraid dissipation cannot withstand a good Scottish education in kirk and school forever. We try, some of us, but our hearts are never really in it. There is always some minister in the background, warning of eternal damnation. It makes me a particularly strenuous sort of Catholic. I am of a Jansenist disposition, half a step away from flagellation and birch rods. The Sacred Heart appeals, that wounded and bleeding organ, dripping with grief for the sins of others. It fills me with a guilty pleasure at the suffering and agony I have put our Saviour through.

I take satisfaction from being cold, from having to bathe outside in icy water in winter. The people hereabouts think I am mad, but in truth the winters are not so harsh in comparison to Scotland; I earn my reputation on the cheap. Besides, I am not really concerned about the present; my eyes are fixed on the hereafter.

You do look embarassed. You are convinced that I have lost my reason; that I have sunk into a religious mania which is but one stop from the asylum. Not so; I do not mean my place in heaven, because if that is not already lost to me, it will be, soon enough. I mean my posthumous reputation.

Oh no! You'd prefer the religious fervour, wouldn't you? Better that than the hopeless dreaming of the disappointed, convinced that posterity will see what the contemporary does not. I have been many things in my life, but never pathetic, never an object of sympathy. Is that what exile has reduced me to?

I notice that you do not rush to reassure. You do not smile and say, "Of course! Sooner or later the world will see your true worth. Think of Cézanne, think of van Gogh. . . ." Because you know that is not the case; or you hope not, because that would mean defeat for you and all those very

different people you champion. I would never be one of
your Post-Impressionists. I am further away from them now
than ever. You would rather have your old friend consigned
to a footnote in your own biography than have him accorded
any recognition. You have decided where the high road of
artistic progress is heading and I am merely a branch off it, a
diversion slowly clogging with weeds from neglect, soon to
be overgrown and forgotten entirely.

But still, I am right, not you. And you are going to be the
means of re-establishing my reputation. You said it yourself,
did you not? All those years ago, when you were justifying
your decision to become a critic. The painter without the
critic is nothing. The good critic can make the mediocre famous, the great obscure. His power is limitless; the artist is
his servant, and one day will recognise the fact. And you
were right; you proved it in the way you straddled the galleries, the collectors, the patrons and the journals, whisper-
ing to each, hinting and guiding. Who dared stand against
you? Who even thought they needed to?

I am not accusing you. You never did me any harm,
professionally speaking. Quite the contrary. You cosseted
and protected me, encouraged me always. Take the great exhibition of 1910 when you introduced those wretched Post-
Impressionists into England. The latest French fashion,

brought over by yourself to whack the English in the eye, shock them out of their somnolence, shake them out of their complacency. Only a few—a very select few—English painters were invited to show their pictures alongside those august new masters. And I was one of them. How kind of you. How generous you were, always were.

I still remember every detail of that evening when you came and asked me to take part. You sent my model packing, then got out a small hamper of food and champagne. Laid it out and opened the bottle.

"So what great accomplishment are we to celebrate?" I asked. "Or have you finally realised my true worth as an artist and come to pay homage?"

"Both and neither," you replied with a smile. Not quite a grin—you never let yourself go so far—but close enough. "I am going to pull off the biggest explosion in the history of British art. And I need your help."

And then you laid out what you were going to do. Bring over pictures by Cézanne, Seurat, van Gogh, Degas, mix them in with a few—a select few—English artists who could stand the company, and open the doors.

"With no preparation? No warning? The reviews will be terrible. Atrocious. You won't sell anything. You'll be a laughing stock," I said.

And you laughed again; genuinely this time. "Of course. It will be a catastrophe. If I don't get the worst notices in history, then I shall be severely disappointed. I even intend to write some of them myself, to be published anonymously. 'Never in the history of art has such rubbish been offered up to insult the public sensibility. . . .' That sort of thing. That's the point, don't you see?"

"No."

"Think, man! What have we talked about all these years? About the feebleness of taste in these islands. About how the Good British Public wouldn't know a masterpiece if it was served up to them for breakfast with eggs and bacon."

"True enough."

"And think how everybody agrees with that. Not just you and me and other artists. But everybody. The only universal feature of British art is agreement on how dreadful the public is."

"Agreed."

"So what is the point of trying to get good reviews? If people like it, it proves that it is no good. The only way to ensure long-term success is for it to be absolutely detested. That is the test in modern art. Has been since Manet; has been since Whistler sued when he was accused of throwing a paint pot in the public's face. Which he shouldn't have done. He should have worn it as a badge of pride. It showed what an old-fashioned man he really was. Artists should no longer seek fame. They must seek notoriety. . . ."

Oh, it was grand. There we were, *la vie de Bohème*, you skinny as ever and me with a middle-aged paunch beginning to show, getting slowly more drunk, damning the very people whose money we were angling to transfer into our pockets, agreeing on everything. Paris revisited, for the last time. But you were still in control, were you not? I sat on the floor, you occupied the chair, sitting bolt upright, speaking so quietly I had to strain forward to hear you. I drank too much, you maintained your self-control as ever. "If I don't get the worst reviews . . ." "My pictures . . ." "My show . . ." Where was poor old Cézanne in this? Merely the artisan producing the goods for you to launch your attack with, it seems. And me? Less than that. Would I send some pictures to be included?

"Of course. You can have my portrait of . . ."

"No, no. I will choose. I will choose what best compliments the other ones, if you don't mind. . . ."

Wonderful. Exhilarating. But. But. The Post-Impressionists weren't the latest French fashion, were they? Matisse and Picasso were already going beyond them. You pulled the wool over our eyes. Little did we know that things had already moved on. You knew, of course. You knew everything. But all those newfangled doctrines were too much even for you. The limits to your radicalism showed you up as the conservative you really were, and instead you set up as a confidence trickster, selling old goods as new. How pathetic you made us all seem, even as you were shocking us.

And how pathetic you made me seem as well, and all the other English painters who fell into your trap. We thought we were there to derive glory by association, to become identified with the latest in art. But no. That was not the point, was it? It was an exercise in power that you put on; we were there to show how backward English art was. Anyone with advanced tastes would look at what you had brought over from France, and look at what we were doing, and draw their own conclusions. I wondered why you chose those particular paintings of mine. The portrait of the Countess of Albemarle's gardener; the landscape in Hyde Park. The picture of that ridiculous little dog I painted for your wife. I offered to show you some others, even my dockyard scenes and some of my little whores, but you refused them.

It was a wonderful success. A trumpet blast. Anyone who wanted the latest would have to go to you; you were the gatekeeper of the modern. And if I ever did show my dark pictures, what would have been the result? I would have been congratulated on learning so swiftly from the new art you had brought in. You stole my originality, sir. Reduced me to a cheap imitator of your French friends.

I laughed about it, of course, not least because my pictures were admired and you didn't manage to unload a single Cézanne. A cheap and pyrrhic victory on my part; the more I sold, the more my reputation would eventually sink. Not that I realised that immediately, of course. It was Mrs. Algernon Roberts who pointed it out to me. No? Not one of your circle? I'm not surprised. She is—or was—a large, amiable woman who rides a horse and has a backside which resembles one. Her husband owns a large part of Suffolk, I believe, and in eight generations the family has read two books. Both about hunting. She gardens, badly, and tries to marry her daughter off to rich men, also with little success. She is also—I must add in the interests of accuracy—a charming and generous woman, kind and gentle. Not your sort at all, as I'm sure you will agree.

Anyway, that evening, your opening. She came along. I don't know why; someone must have invited her as a joke. She was dressed in her best and looked as though she'd just emerged from a palace ball. She was wandering around looking utterly bewildered by all those pictures you'd hung up—she whose idea of artistic radicalism is Constable—and then saw me. We had met through one of her friends, whom I'd painted a year or so previously. She had arrived in mid-sitting and insisted on watching me at work. I was a bit hard up at the time and thought it might lead to a commission, which it might have, had I not come here. So I let her sit behind me and found her presence oddly congenial. Unlike her friend, who kept on rushing round to see what I was doing and making imbecilic remarks—so much so that I felt like taking off my belt and strapping her to her chair—she sat quietly and watched. "It's like birthing a horse," she said cheerfully—and quite appropriately, considering what her friend looked like. "The beast needs all its concentration."

The remark was so ridiculous it was almost wise; and I took to her, and she to me. I could hardly say we became friends, as we had nothing in common whatsoever, but across that great divide the English language creates to keep people separate, we recognised a certain fellow-feeling. She was the sort of person who would make you a cup of tea and put you up for a month if anything bad ever happened. Reassuring, and I don't know many people like that.

Anyway, that evening she sailed across the room with a view-halloo when she saw me. "How lovely to see a friendly face," she said. "Everybody here looks so cross. And your paintings, too. Why, they look as out of place as I feel."

On the nail. She had an intuitive intelligence far beyond my range. She saw, she commented, and never let any analytical process interfere with the immediacy of her opinions. She was a sort of intellectual Impressionist, if you like, slapping down raw insight with a freshness that was almost unnerving in that overcerebral world. I fear her wisdom was not received with the appreciation that was its due that evening, as the words hit me in the stomach like a punch. All of a sudden I was no longer part of an eager company of progressive painters, part of the new radicalism. I was a stranger in a crowd, whose only human contact was a female equestrian of uncertain age from Suffolk.

I think I was probably quite rude to her; made some dismissive remark, turned away. But she was right; I had spent much of my time assailing the old fogeys of art and suddenly discovered, thanks to you, that I was to be one myself. This was the fate you had laid out for me.

HAVE YOU EVER noticed that no artist has ever committed cold-blooded murder? In the whole history of art, go back as

far as you can, and no artist has ever been a true killer. Oh, I
know, there have been accidents, like Caravaggio stabbing
someone in a fight, but that hardly counts. And many kill
themselves. But what I mean is deliberate intent, a planned
murder. This we do not do. Why is this, do you think? Is it
because we are creators, not destroyers? Is it because—as all
the world knows who truly understands—that we are really
feeble, frightened characters for all our bluster, more keen
on being accepted and praised than wreaking vengeance on
others?

Whatever the reason, it is true. And think again; what a
wonderful defence it would be in a court of law. Suppose I
were to push someone off a cliff, and suppose I were clever
enough to make sure no-one saw me do it. Suppose, nonetheless, the police built a case against me. Imagine the scene in
the courtroom. All the reporters, the jury, the judge, the
lawyers, all focussed on the witness box. And me, standing
there, grand, disdainful, slightly flamboyant to indicate my
bohemianism, but not so much that I antagonise the jury.
Dear Lord, the speech I could make! Oscar would have
bowed his head in submission to my superiority; Whistler
would, for once, have acknowledged one greater than he.

"Do you think that any individual could distract me from
my art? Men die; an artist is a creator of the eternal. Do you

think we would demean ourselves with the transient?" And so on. You see the strategy? It would not be me, but the whole of art that would be in the dock. A jury might find me guilty; I doubt they would have the temerity to find Cimabue, Raphael, Michelangelo, Gainsborough and Turner guilty as well. They would stand beside me, shoulder to shoulder. One for all and all for one. "Look at my works and see the soul within; could someone whose life is dedicated to the pursuit of Truth and Beauty contemplate the squalid and the violent. . . ." The jurors would take me on trust. You are not the only one capable of exploiting the English sense of inferiority in this regard. Only a painter could use such a strategy and get away with it. If you were a fishmonger you wouldn't prepare a defence that relied on the fact that few fishmongers have violent tendencies, although for all I know they may be very pacific. But with a painter I believe you could do it, and easily.

Perhaps it is not true, in any case. Perhaps artists kill their fellow men all the time, but do it so well they get away with it. Our humiliation of you over that fake I kept to myself; a murder, I suspect, would be as easily concealed. But, of course, I would have to reveal it eventually, just as I eventually told you about your Gauguin. I would leave an account in my papers, to be read at some stage after my final demise.

Not a confession, but a justification, as I would have to be entirely justified in my acts.

But what motive could any painter have for killing? The usual reasons are not good enough. Jealousy, greed, shame; the holy trinity of death. These account for nearly all murders, I think, and pretty trivial they are, when you come to consider them. What about art, though? Could we murder for that? A bad idea, really. Who would we choose? Bad painters? There would be a bloodbath. Stupid patrons? The streets would be littered with corpses. A critic or two? Maybe; there is no love lost between us. A critic is to a painter as a eunuch is to a man, so the saying goes. But that doesn't stop us running after you, does it? Doesn't mean we refuse to invite you to our shows. Somebody must do the dirty business, and you have that task. We even accept that you are not there to boost our careers, that your job is to foster art itself, and so can take a bad review—as long as it is not we who get them. As long as the critic is the honest servant of art, we will have to live together.

Anderson did not murder you, even though you destroyed his life, took away his dreams and turned him into an art dealer. He could not; he had no right, and he knew it. Because you spoke the truth, however harshly and malevolently. You were not giving your opinion only. Delphi was sacrosanct to the Greeks, no matter what the oracles said. The priestess communicated the words of Apollo, not her own; she was merely a messenger. So were you with Anderson. It was not your fault he was no good. He could and did hate you for the pleasure you took in it, but not for telling the truth. You had the perfect protection, an inpenetrable suit of armour to ward off any danger. As long as you had that defence, you were invulnerable.

But what if you lost that defence? What if your cruelty and ruthlessness turned into promoting and defending yourself, rather than art? What if you began to destroy good painters and encourage inferior ones for your own advancement only? Would then legions of angry painters beat their way to your door, hammer it down and administer justice? It is impossible to imagine; for who could tell where the lies began?

So, no murders there, at least not yet. A pity, in some ways. It would be a peculiar sensation; one which is no longer respectable, of course, but which all ages before us have venerated as one of the highest human activities. Now only governments kill, and they have become properly efficient at the task. Only politicians know the sensation of taking human life—which, you must admit, is a bad thing for painting as so many subjects involve death or violence. How can one depict it if one has not experienced it? How can one appreciate it if one does not know it at first hand?

WHEN I MAKE all these sniffy remarks about the French, I do not mean to denigrate them, you know. Fine to be French; it is the *faux-français* that revolt me. Paris was a good time, my liberation. Not as a painter, as I learned next to nothing there and had to spend years getting rid of what I did absorb. But as a man, it was crucial. I went there nervous, shy, uncomfortable, and came back—myself. In all my ostentatious glory, swaggering around the London stage proclaiming myself. I became a character, what the artist should be. It was only a stage show, but worked well enough as that. Some hated me, and thought me fraud or fool, some found me entertaining. But everybody noticed me; and that is the key to success in the world these days. Far more important than actually being good. To impose yourself, to take the public by the scruff of the neck and give it a good shaking; to scream in its provincial little ear that *I am a genius*. And if you scream loud enough and long enough, it believes you. Establish that, and in the public mind a good painting becomes a masterpiece, a failure becomes a bold experiment. I saw that in Paris, and learned how to shout.

You watched my transfiguration and guided it; I can remember how it felt, when the penny dropped. It was in a bar, not far from the atelier, and there was a group of us talking. A long day's work, our eyes still tired from strain, the smell of paint and turpentine hanging over us. Each of us marked by our filthy, blackened fingernails, multicoloured hands. The exuberance of noisy conversation after a hard day, for we were serious, you know. We worked hard eight, ten, sometimes twelve hours a day in summer, learning our craft and trying to equip ourselves for the battles to come, when we had to put it into practise. I can't remember who was there; Rothenstein for one, I imagine, prim and proper as he always was, making his pursed and always slightly flattening comments, taking the joy out of the occasion by always insisting on thinking about what he said. McAvoy, perhaps, with his disconcerting habit of interjecting a comment that had nothing to do with what we were talking about. Evelyn was certainly not there; she packed her bags at the end of the day and went home. She was always a thing apart, never one of a group. We were drinking and I could not take my drink;

my puritan blood was not used to it. A little went a long way, and after two glasses I was roaring drunk while everyone else was still stone cold sober. My tongue loosened, and I said something perfectly absurd; the sort of thing that my normal self would never have dared think, let alone say.

I can't remember what it was, but I remember the formula: take any major artist and stress a weakness, real or imagined. Build yourself up by diminishing others greater than yourself. The critic's trick. So what was it? Manet would be a great artist if only he could control his line. Rembrandt's lack of structure precludes him from being considered a true genius. Raphael's weakness was that he lacked a Venetian's sense of colour. Some nonsense like that. And to my surprise I found people nodding, not daring to make the obvious response that I was talking rubbish. Not because they agreed with me, either; but because I had spoken with such vehemence. I was allowed to say drivel, even encouraged to do so. I had come into my birthright.

I felt ashamed of myself, and even more ashamed of those who didn't stop me, but it was a touch of power, and out of that moment grew the artist I became. I learned to impose myself, force myself on other people, bully them with my presence and my convictions and, in so doing, convince my-

self as well. I became a boor and found that people flocked
to me, wanting me to do violence to them or, if not that, to
be around while I assaulted others.

Except for prissy little Evelyn, of course, who missed my
artistic birth in the bar. I took her out one evening, in Paris.
She was lonely, and I decided she was ripe for assault. I
would attack, overwhelm and achieve a grand victory over
her. What was she, after all? I wanted to try out my new per-
sona on an easy target, and she seemed perfect for it. I was
even prepared to spend money, although getting others to
spend it for me soon became a part of my reputation. It is
strange how others feel in your debt if they pay for you in
restaurants.

It wasn't high elegance, though, that evening. We went to
a *bouillon* which I liked because it was the Paris of the people,
the sort of place where not even English painters could be
found. No tablecloths, waiters even rougher than the clien-
tele, mainly used by people without any means of cooking
themselves who ate *en pension* there, keeping their knives in
their own wooden box by the entrance. I frequented many
of them, but my favourite was down by Bercy, where you
could sit next to the wine men and hear the accents of Bur-
gundy and Bordeaux. The whole place stank of rancid wine
and sweat from their clothes, but the food wasn't bad and

the wine was better than you get in many a fine restaurant. No women there at all, ever: this was a place for men to eat.

That was part of my plan, of course, the first stage in my scheme to intimidate. Evelyn, I decided, would be so scared of being in such a place that she would look to me, would shrink against me in that hostile, violent place. I would become her protector, and once that was established, all else would be easy.

It started well, because she dressed in her best for the occasion. Not elegantly, of course, she had no good clothes in that sense. Plain, comfortable garb, almost masculine in style which she rescued from ugliness with a touch of colour or detail—she somehow managed to make an artificial flower in her hair seem charming, a cheap necklace seem stylish. She had a way of putting things together on her body which suggested a sensuality which was the more intriguing for being so carefully hidden. Something she wanted to advertise but was afraid of at the same time. It was what made her so proper and seemingly so mousy, until you got to know her and realised she was nothing of the sort.

I had not reckoned, of course, on her ability to call on the inherent sense of superiority of the middle-class English female to protect her in hostile territory. She comes from the class of women who made the empire, who can sail through the much more unfriendly waters of a charity bazaar or Park Lane tea party and emerge unscathed. Half a hundred burly French drunks are as nothing to such people; in fact, she blossomed under the challenge. All her natural shyness vanished as she settled into a role she understood all too well. She sat down at her table, and straightaway asked the man next to her—an enormous, scowling Parisian who could have crushed her in one giant paw—if he would be so kind as to stop smoking.

A silence fell. Someone sniggered, but stopped dead when she fixed him with a steely glance and slightly raised eyebrow. The cigarette was dropped to the floor and crushed out with the heel of a huge boot. The conversation resumed once more and, now that Evelyn had established herself as the hostess of our little table, she held court for the rest of the evening, genteelly receiving compliments and, it seemed, quite enjoying herself. Every five minutes, a fresh glass of wine would be presented to us by our new friends, then the cognac merchants weighed in and a tide of brandy rolled over us, propelled by the irresistible force of amiable sentiment. Her French was much better than mine; I became her companion, tolerated because I was with her, not the other way round.

The end was inevitable; Evelyn, I discovered, could drink even a stevedore under the table. She came from a long line of heavy drinkers and it seemed to have no effect on her. You remember what it did to me. My plans were in disarray; I was humiliated, exposed as a fraud—and I knew that she saw, and understood, everything. She all but had to carry me out, and when, in my befuddled state, I hurled myself on her, she sidestepped daintily and I fell, heavily, onto the ground. It took me some time to get up again, and when I rolled over I saw her sitting on a stone wall looking at me as though I was a six-year-old who'd just dropped some chocolate on the Wilton.

Somehow or other she got me back to my lodgings and left me propped up at the door; during the whole evening we'd barely said a word to each other. She'd talked to the warehousemen while I'd slowly descended into a black, drunken depression.

"Listen, Henry MacAlpine," she said as she left me. "You cannot take your drink very well. You really shouldn't try; it doesn't bring out the best in you." Then she patted me affectionately on the shoulder and walked off.

And that was the end of the adventure. You laugh; yes. I laugh myself now, although at the time I found it anything but funny. You, no doubt, would never have allowed such a thing to happen to you. But then you don't know anything at all about humiliation. You don't know what it is to have your weaknesses and stupidities dragged out for public view, to be treated gently even though you deserve mockery. There I have the advantage of you; it is something we lowland Scots specialise in. We are ready to be humiliated, almost invite it, and welcome it with relief when it comes. It proves that God is watching us, that daily his judgement continues.

It didn't matter that Evelyn was the only person ever to do that to me. Somebody existed in the world who could see through me, and stopped me from believing in my new self totally. As long as I remembered that, I knew that Henry MacAlpine, artist, was nothing more than a piece of fakery, a theatrical production designed merely to sell second-rate pictures to a foolish public.

What I mean to say here is that I had very good reason to hate Evelyn. Had I done so I could have stood before the Lord (in due course) with my hand on my heart and pleaded self-justification. Twice she wounded me in my *amour propre*; she humiliated me, pitied me and rejected me, and on all occasions did it with kindness. Wars have started for less reason than that.

She never did anything of the sort to you. With you she

was always distant but polite, too withdrawn and too inexperienced in the ways of the world even to deserve much attention from you.

So why was it that you hated her, and I did not? That is a mystery, is it not?

❧

LOOKING BACK from my vantage point by the wide Atlantic, I can see that Evelyn had irritated you from the moment you first cast eyes on her at Julien's. There was something about her determination, her resolution, that annoyed you. Already she was going her own way, carefully learning what she wanted to learn, not what everyone else was doing. She decided to have a go at lithography, even though it was the lowest of all art forms. Little better than being a grubby printer turning out stock catalogues for department stores, so you thought. You didn't realise then that the next generation of French painters—your generation, the ones who have made your name for you—would discover it as well, and use it to good effect. Nor did she, of course; she was utterly indifferent to any such information. She merely became fascinated by the possibilities of drawing straight onto a piece of limestone, and wanted to see what could be done with it.

Being so direct, she took herself off, went to one of those printers you so despised, and sat at his feet for several months as though he had been Rubens himself. He knew things she wanted to learn, and her sense of dignity was so great she felt it no shame to go to mere artisans for instruction. And she learned, by God, better than any of us. Did you respect her the more for it? Of course not. Did I? No; I followed your lead, and forgot how much such people can know, and how much they can teach. I had been one myself, after all; the same people had taught me, too, and taught me well. And in my effort to put all my past behind me, to forget the workshop in Glasgow, I scorned her as much as you did.

Or was it the lack of gentility and decorum, to think of her with her hands covered in ink, straining to pull the heavy roller over the stone? Shouldn't such people be in the drawing room? Should such dainty little muscles be used only for pouring tea? Shouldn't that look of satisfaction come only from hearing a husband make some witty remark? Of course they should! The woman was an aberration, a freak, to desire such things and take pleasure in them. But she did so desire them, and the pleasure was real.

I remember once she disappeared for a few days; I think maybe I was the only one who noticed; this was a few months after my humiliation at the *bouillon* in Bercy. Eventually, I went round to her lodgings and persuaded the ogre who owned them to let me go up and see her. She was ill with a flu, and had a terrible bronchitic cough; I thought when I heard her she might be consumptive. But no; it was just a cough, but a bad one, poor dear, made worse by having had no attention at all for several days. She was in a mess, but too proud to ask for help. Perhaps she thought no-one liked her, and didn't want an appeal for help ignored. Foolish of her; she was liked more than she realised. She made people nervous, of course, but there were some able to conquer such emotions. I can't say that illness made her more attractive; with some, the onset of frailty and vulnerability makes you want to sweep them up in your arms, cosset them and protect them. Many a woman has snared a husband with a well-timed burst of fainting. Not Evelyn. Weakness made her almost repulsive; her skin turned sallow rather than pale, and she lay curled up like some sort of insect. Take away the movement and she had no natural grace; she was awkward, ungainly and uncoordinated unless she was holding a brush or pencil. It seemed the only thing that could bring her alive.

Anyway, she was crying; I thought it was just the sickness, and I've no doubt that did make it worse, but the real reason was that she hadn't been able to draw or paint since she fell sick. The previous day she had become so desperate she

tried to get to the desk by the little window to draw something, anything. "It's like an addiction," she said. "I go mad if
I can't use my hands. It's all I have, the only thing that makes
it worthwhile getting out of bed in the morning."

Do you understand that? I do, just. I feel it sometimes but
not with the intensity of her affliction. It was like breathing
for her. Take it away and she began to feel stifled. Neurosis?
Hysteria? I've no doubt. I'm sure some infection of the
uterus was behind it all. Or, if that is out of favour now,
some physiological imbalance in her brain. No doubt, nothing that a baby or two wouldn't have cured. But like a man
who drags himself off to some squalid opium hell for his
pipe and secretly relishes the prospect as much as he is disgusted by himself, she didn't want to be cured. She didn't
want the madness taken away from her. It was her most treasured possession. It was what she was, and it made her both
magnificent and, as you say, a freak.

I remember you tried to convert her at one stage, to bring
her in as your disciple. If Jesus could put up with Mary Mag-
dalene, it was not beneath you to have a woman or two in
your entourage. She should have been more flattered, I
grant you. No-one has ever doubted your eye, and you have
never put up with fools or the second rate. It gives the lie to
your later opinions, you know. She was not to be mere orna-

ment; that has never been your failing. It is part of your egotism that only the best should be allowed to surround you. And you tried to lure Evelyn to your side. I rest my case.

So you invited her to your soirées in Paris, to meet the people she should really know; not the printers and their assistants, but the men with power and influence. To take tea with Proust, with Oscar Wilde, with Anatole France. With *salonnières* and novelists and politicians, with other artists, but only those carefully selected. How did you know all these people, anyway? I never figured it out. How did you have the self-confidence to invite them and expect them to show up? You were nothing but a bumptious little Englishman with some skill at conversation. Some connections, but nothing special. Charm, I suppose; you managed to make people think you were a good investment for the future. Of course I was jealous. Why should I not be? It was so easy for you, so hard for me. It wasn't until I realised that brooding ill-humour had its own appeal that I could stop making myself ridiculous.

Anyway, into this society of the great, you invited Evelyn, along with some other candidates for patronage. I expected her to be cowed, grateful, a little obviously trying to make a good impression. Giving off all those signs of someone ill at ease—perched on the edge of her chair, nervous of speech either too loud or too soft. Saying little, but listening carefully to every one else. As I did when you invited me.

Certainly she didn't say much, but what she did say was to the point. Don't pretend you don't remember what she said to Sarah Bernhardt; I know full well it is ingrained in your memory. She announced in a clear voice that the great lady's opinion on some painting was facile; that perhaps she should look more and opine less. But *lèse-majesté,* no? Evelyn was there to worship and admire, not to treat these people as equals, and certainly not to criticise them. I can still remember the smooth way you intervened and changed the topic of conversation, showing how capable you were even in awkward situations.

But I can also remember the look on La Bernhardt's face: a look of boredom dissipated. Splendid woman, as vain as a peacock but knows how to tell the difference between praise and flattery. She is a professional, after all; her success depends on being able to distinguish the two. She knew she'd been caught out, that the comment was justified. She liked being assaulted by this skinny little girl who tossed her head with a sort of naïve defiance and looked you in the eye as she spoke. It spiced up the dull fare of adulation that was her normal lot. All those gasps of amazement, that delight in whatever she said, the squeaks of appreciation at her slightest utterance. Someone like Evelyn must have been like a glass of cold fresh water after an afternoon drinking undiluted treacle.

How much did it grieve you when Evelyn was invited to supper and you never were? Don't pretend; you were furious. I know you too well to pretend otherwise. Even more so when you realised that she was not in the slightest bit gratified by the honour. She went, she ate, she had a "perfectly nice time, thank you." She was impervious to such things, and so she was impervious to you, as well. She did not want to be around the famous. You in particular had nothing to offer her, except for your skills in society, your politician's ability to make people do your bidding, so she stopped coming to your little gatherings. It wasn't meant to be insulting, you know. She did not realise that she had delivered an irreparable insult, had struck at the core of your power. She rejected you even more completely than she rejected me.

A few friends, the rest enemies. That was your philosophy of life, and Evelyn showed she did not want to be your friend.

"Surely, a painting works or it doesn't, no?" That was her response after you had laid out an early version of your theory of art, of modernity, of the artistic engagement with reality and all the rest of it. It was naïve, unsophisticated, but a damning indictment of your whole life's work, which seeks to make things more complex and obscure, more difficult to understand. To turn a simple pleasure into a mystery. For Evelyn, there was the painting and the viewer; a direct communion. She was an artistic protestant, and had no need of intermediaries, be they critics or priests.

Her weakness was the crippling self-doubt that afflicted her every step of the way. That is the price of Protestantism and individuality. The constant worry of having to choose between good and bad fades when you cede authority to others. That is probably why I was so eager to bow to your judgement, and why I am such a happy papist. Having to make up your own mind is a terrible burden, and the inevitable cost is massive doubt.

I didn't realise it until I had a terrible fight with her one day; you sensed it instinctively, knew where to strike when the moment came. That was well after we all drifted back to London for the new century. I started painting portraits, and desperately began seeking publicity—any publicity—to become known. Any exhibition that would accept my pictures got them in abundance. Any notice in the press was pored over and treasured. I sent picture after picture to the RA, and had most of them turned down. In my clodhopping way, I cultivated those who might be of use to me somehow. I was a desperate man; this was my last throw. Until then I had been able to persuade myself I was still young, still learning. Now I was past thirty and I knew I would not get much better, and I was not sure if Anderson's fate awaited me. I needed all the help I could get and wasn't too proud to ask for it. Especially as you encouraged me, and told me it was the only way to succeed.

Evelyn did none of it. When she finally came back in 1902 she contacted nobody, took lodgings in Clapham and was scarcely ever seen. I didn't even realise she'd returned until she'd been back nearly a year. I felt quite insulted by that, and thought that she disdained all the little humiliations I put myself to because she could afford to. Her father was a barrister, I remember, and I imagined he supported her. An artistic daughter, how charming! She never mentioned that they disapproved so thoroughly that they gave her not one ha'penny; wouldn't even talk to her. There is, after all, a difference between painting pictures and being an artist. She freely gave up everything I wanted—house, money, comfort. The only hot food she ever ate was in the cheap working men's cafés in the area, or unless someone took her out for a free meal. Most of the little money she had she spent on canvasses and paints. But she more or less managed to keep up appearances, proper girl that she was, and was too proud to glory in her poverty or play the bohemian. It was the way it was; no choice. It took someone who knew her well to realise she had been wearing the same clothes when she arrived in Paris, or to see the exquisite stitching that had repaired a threadbare patch here, or a little hole there. We were travelling in opposite directions, she and I.

I didn't know how she did it. I would have withered in similar circumstances. It's all very well being wedded to your art, but *someone* has to notice. Someone has to approve, or appreciate, or buy. No-one is so sublimely confident that they can do without any applause, however faint and sporadic. But Evelyn rarely showed her pictures, scarcely ever sold one. I hadn't seen anything she'd produced for years. She was entirely unknown, forgotten by most of those she knew in Paris, not taken seriously by anyone else. Most people didn't even know she painted. It didn't appear to have any effect on her. Indeed, she seemed to thrive on it; around that time I'd noticed a fire in her eyes, a self-confidence that almost seemed like happiness, I had never seen in Paris.

She didn't encourage visitors; we met in cafés usually, occasionally in my studio, but after about five years I needed to get hold of her; I'd sold a picture to the Countess of Armagh, and I needed to celebrate with someone as a matter of urgency. I planned to spend some of my fee in advance, and take her for a good meal. She needed the food, and I needed the company; she was one of the few painters I knew who would be able to listen to my bragging without feeling impatient or envious. Besides, I relied on her to bring me back down to earth when the vainglory got wearisome, by asking whether the picture I'd sold was actually worth the money.

So I took a cab to Clapham—which shows how opulent I was feeling—and arrived on her doorstep. And got a shock: her lodgings were even more mean than Jacky's. Freezing, bitterly cold. She was out when I arrived, but the landlady was an amiable woman and, as it was even colder outside than in, let me in to wait. The room—on the top floor of a building which smelt strongly of boiled vegetables and floor polish—was tiny and had scarcely any furniture in it, just a grate, a bed, a chair and a table. It was lit—when it was lit— by a remarkably ornate chandelier hanging from a vast iron hook in the middle of the ceiling. Heavens knows how it got there. That was all, apart from the pictures—dozens of them, all stacked against the wall, piles of paper on the one little desk and on the floor, boxes of paints, bottles of solvents. The usual stuff, but an awful lot of it.

I started looking at the pictures. Of course I did; who wouldn't? It never occurred to me not to. Every painter who ever came into my studio in Hammersmith went through the canvasses as a matter of course to see what I was up to. I did the same myself, wherever I went. Nosiness is the great driving force of art. Think of Raphael sneaking into the Sistine Chapel to see what his great rival was up to. In Evelyn's little room I was astonished by what I saw; truly I was. You weren't there to guide me, and I had seen nothing by her hand for ages. She had achieved a remarkable simplicity. One particularly stayed with me: a picture of her little wicker chair against the window. That was it; nothing else in the image at all, but it was delightful, warm and lonely, confident and despairing, simple and subtle. Such a mixture of differing emotions and reflections it threw up, it was quite dazzling. And tiny as well—not more than ten inches square. As near to perfection as you can get. She'd taken the spirit of someone like Vermeer and turned it into something wholly modern and personal. Exquisite.

I was looking at it when she came in, and instantly forgot all about wicker chairs. She was furious with me, and I had never seen her truly angry before. Nothing had ever got through the quiet, well-brought-up behaviour that made her so easy to underestimate. "How dare you go through my private things? Who do you think you are. . . ." Her rage was like a torrent that swept over me, terrifying in its intensity, the more so for being so completely unexpected.

And much much more. She was deeply offended, but more than that: she was terrified. As she bustled about, collecting the few pictures I had looked at, carefully stacking them once more with their faces to the wall so they could not be seen, I suddenly realised she was embarrassed; she thought I might make some critical remark, might make fun of her for painting a chair in a bedroom. Good heavens, that was the last thing that occurred to me. But she would not listen to any of my attempts to reassure, or even apologise. She was near to tears with fury; anyone would have thought I had made an indecent advance. By her lights I suppose I had, far more than in Paris. I had violated her privacy, and exposed her weakness—she put everything into those pictures, and she was afraid of what others might see in them. Still, I wished I had seen more, wished I could have seen the ones she particularly did not want me to look at.

She threw me out, and I had to write a grovelling letter—a long one—to win forgiveness. Even so, she didn't speak to me for months and still wouldn't talk about it, although I tried. "What's the point of painting the wretched things if no-one ever sees them?" I tried saying once.

"They're not ready. They're not good enough and I don't want to talk about it. . . ."

But eventually, she was forced to decide. I forced her. The Chenil gallery offered her a show, largely because I had enthused to them and piqued their interest. They decided to take a risk on a woman whose paintings they had never even seen. Imagine how good that made me feel! That I could exert such influence, that my word alone could conjure such things into existence. There was a bit of politics involved, of course. They wanted to put on an exhibition of Augustus John, but he had pulled out because the dates coincided with your big Post-Impressionism display. Not only was he mortally offended he'd not been invited by you, he was clever enough to realise that the furore you were going to cause would swamp everything else. So the Chenil had the prospect of blank walls for a couple of weeks. A little show by an unknown artist, which wouldn't be seen as a defeat if it failed to get much attention, was just what they needed.

So they came to her. She hesitated, because she knew what accepting meant. It meant dropping the pretence of disdaining the opinion of outsiders. An exhibition means you do care what other people think. You do want their good opinion. And in order to get it you make yourself public, and invite comments, good and bad. You cannot keep up the illusion that you are merely trying to satisfy yourself. You sign a pact with the devil.

I pushed her, I admit it, and not for her sake. I had my own reputation to think of, and John Knewstub from the Chenil had made the approach on my recommendation. Besides, the couple of pictures I had seen *were* good. A damned sight better than many of the things that go on show. They were crying out to be seen, to have their chance. It was cruel to keep them locked up. Paintings are creatures of the open air; they need to breathe, to have attention to stop them withering. Crammed in the basement of a museum, or an art gallery or turned to face the wall in a studio, they die a little. It is not why they exist.

YOU'VE MANAGED to make yourself unpopular on this island already, you know. I have had words. The priest asked when you were leaving. A raised eyebrow from one of the fishermen. They are subtle people here; they never say something if they can communicate it in any other way. I tried to figure out what you have done to irritate, then decided that your mere existence was probably enough, although refusing to pay court to Father Charles probably helped. Are you so great that you will not submit yourself to boredom for even half an hour in order to create the right impression? The air of disdain which is such a useful tool in a metropolis is of little use here. They do not want you to be ingratiating, to engage them in conversation, or show an interest in their lives, of course. It would be a mistake to offer them a drink; that is their privilege, not yours. They can spot the difference between friendliness and condescension before even a foot is placed on the quayside. I had to wait nearly a year before my patience was rewarded with a nod in the road or a muttered comment about the weather. If I stayed another twenty years they would still be suspicious of me. They are poor, largely uneducated, and simple, by your lights and mine. But you should not make the mistake of considering them inconsequential, and I fear that the way you habitually insulate yourself from the outside world, the manner in which you look at people as though they were contained in an ornate frame, has not been a great hit. Rather than inspiring awe and a little fear, of disconcerting people and making them more malleable, it has had the opposite effect. They are stiff-necked, and proud, and need to be courted.

Deserve to be courted, I should say, because they can live

in this place; you could not. They will not harm you, of course, you are not worth it to them. But you would never be able to go to them for help, or assistance. When you wish to go back to the mainland, it will be through my intercession, otherwise you would find that all the boats are much too busy. You are fed and lodged because I have requested it, otherwise you would starve on the beach. Should you fall ill or sustain an injury, any treatment you receive will be at my behest, not yours. You are alone here, and friendless. Apart from me. I wouldn't worry about it too much, though. I was simply trying to alarm you, and remind you that your writ does not run everywhere. Your kingdom runs from Chelsea to Oxford Circus only. Outside that, you are powerless, and reliant on the goodwill of others.

Did I ever tell you of the moment when I decided to become a painter? When I realised that was what I was, in fact? It was in the drawing office, in my third year of apprenticeship in Glasgow. You have no interest in such things, I know, but it was a comradely place; I was not unhappy there. My father had decided he wanted me off his hands, and that I should be put to work, as he put it, earning good money. A trade, in fact, and it says something of him that he chose the best one—despite his apparent lack of interest in me, he could be a thoughtful man to his children, if harsh and un-forgiving as well. He is one of the few people I have ever missed. A lesser parent might have sent me to the shipyards, to become a boilermaker, or apprenticed me in a bank as a clerk. It would have been cheaper, the rewards more sure. Such a place would have killed me. I'm not being dramatic; I mean merely that I would have stayed there and never found the courage to leave. In due course I would have been given my gold watch, and died, and that would have been that.

But he sent me to a drawing office instead, and I worked there until I was near twenty-three. I was absent in spirit for the last two, as I was by then spending every spare evening at the art school and passed the days dreaming of grander things. No matter; my moment of epiphany came at work, when I was not yet seventeen. I had been put to a design for a biscuit tin, a scene of elegant ladies taking tea in a drawing room, servants in the background. Bright and sunny and cheerful. No longer will you be in some little terraced house in the back streets of some grimy industrial suburb. One bite of what lies within and the good life will be yours. That was to be the message of my tin, eventually emblazoned on countless thousands of Messrs Huntley and Palmer's best butter shortbreads. I'd been working on it steadily for days, and suddenly time stopped. At about a quarter past eleven on a cold November morning. When it started again, the tin was finished. My ladies breathed, you could smell the freshly brewed tea, the sun really did shine in through the broad windows, the fire in the grate had a real warmth. You could feel it.

It was, dare I say it, a masterpiece, my first and perhaps only one. Not that that matters; what I am trying to say is that for the first time I knew what prayer was. Not the grim special pleading that still took place at the foot of my bed every night, but a true communion. My mind and my body and my soul all totally committed to the process. There was no difference between them at all. It was a special moment, that one; it may have lasted for a couple of hours in all, and when I was finished my eyes hurt and my back ached and my fingers were so cramped from holding the brush that I had to take them and straighten them out with my other hand. But I was more exhilarated than I had ever been in my life.

There was no-one to tell about it; no-one in that office or at home could possibly understand. But I had changed irrevocably, and my days as a draughtsman and commercial painter were numbered. I knew the difference between painting and creating, the joy of doing something so perfectly that it made sense of everything else. Yes, yes. I see your smile. A biscuit tin. But don't you see? It was a *perfect* biscuit tin. The most perfect biscuit tin ever created. More harmonious, more absolutely a biscuit tin than the mind of man had ever before contemplated. The illustration was in ideal proportion to the tin. The figures were the quintessence of the biscuits themselves, the colouring a summation of the whole and blending perfectly with it. And I had created it, with my hands and eyes and mind working together in absolute peace.

Oh, they liked it, but I didn't get the shilling bonus I'd expected because I had departed from my instructions. Four figures taking tea, they had said. And I had only put in three, because three was all that was needed. Four would have been excessive; would have ruined the whole. They merely thought I was trying to skimp on the work; so no shilling for me. Not that I cared. I knew how good it was, you see, and that was all that mattered then. For a brief moment, I really didn't care what anyone else thought.

And that is what a painter is. Someone who prays with his brush, something the critic can never do and can never properly understand. From that moment, I have wanted to recapture the moment of paradise that I found in that noisy, cold workroom. I've spent the rest of my life chasing it; sometimes coming close, but most of the time missing. For most of the time I have been no different to those journeymen I left behind me. They churn out the biscuit tins, I turned out paintings of rich women. Somewhere, I lost my innocence.

YOU NEVER understood any of this. You thought I wished to escape from my past, put it all behind me and bathe in the fresh air of the cosmopolitan world. Rid myself of the stultifying, cramped pettiness of Scotland. Not so; not entirely. You thought that my progress—after I had met you—was one of growth, turning myself into an artist and a human being, my triumph being all the greater because I didn't allow Scotland to crush me. Nothing is ever so simple, alas.

Let me explain. I told you often about getting up at five every morning in the icy Gorbals lodgings I stayed in, going to work with a slice of dried porridge in my pocket for my lunch; of working with chilblains on my fingers in winter, of never seeing daylight for six months of the year. Working from seven in the morning to seven at night six days a week with four days holiday a year. Turning out drawings of cogs and machinery, architectural plans, biscuit tins, posters— anything that came in. Rarely even knowing what it was for or who it was for. Bleak and joyless, no? Well, no. To you, of course, it is so far removed from anything you have experienced that it must seem so, and I confess I made it sound as grim as possible. I wished to be like you in those days, to feel and think as I ought. But I wasn't really telling the truth. I don't look back on that time of my life with a shudder at all.

Even working for the magazines in London had its enjoyable side, though the work was hard and the pay terrible. Spending an entire day outside the Old Bailey to catch a glimpse of a murder suspect so a sketch could appear to spice up the account, the faces distorted to look properly criminal, is a good training for the portraitist of an impressionist tendency. You work fast, and there is no time for artistic vapours. You see, run off a sketch on the omnibus back to the office, have ten minutes to finish it off, if you're lucky, then off on the next assignment. Not that anybody ever really looked at the result.

There was one man, accused of killing his wife for her inheritance, who had a passing resemblance to the prime minister. Just to see what would happen, I put in a real sketch of Lord Salisbury, complete with hooded eyebrows, high-domed forehead and opulent beard. I even dressed him up in a proper frock coat. "Man charged with brutality and theft," was the headline, and my picture of the prime minister underneath. I waited for laughter, or at least to be dismissed from my post. Scarcely anyone noticed at all, except for my fellow journalists. Those illustrations were just decorations, to break up the monotony of the print. All my labour was there simply to give a little variety to the page, so the reader would not get too bored and start looking out of the window of the omnibus instead.

Don't you also regret the lost enthusiasm of youth? Look back to that time when all was new and fresh, when nothing was known, all was to be discovered? When every joke was classic, every piece of tomfoolery a delight?

Perhaps not; your youth was so different to mine. Certainly I was afraid when I went to that drawing office in Glasgow, even though the relief of leaving home was so great that almost anything was preferable. The size and horror of the big city, the loneliness, the cold, all chilled me. But it was exciting to feel such intensity in the world. Before I had only had such extreme emotions from the inside; only guilt and the fear of God and mother had made me feel so alive.

And I met people such as I never dreamed existed—wastrels always joking and blaspheming; drunks who could do a better job after half a bottle of whisky than most men sober; the occasional bully; the more frequent saint. I became the mascot of them all, just as I became your mascot when I came south. But the difference was that they wanted nothing from me.

They taught me, too. The one thing I had been good at in school was drawing; I could do plans of complicated machines far beyond the capabilities of my fellows at school, but when I got to the workshop I realised I could do almost nothing; that my pride was misplaced. More than anything, it taught me never to think I was finished.

I started learning, as I had never learned before or since. And if I am often scornful of the technical failings of others, it is because I know how hard it is to acquire good technique. I acquired mine by constant labour and study, year after year, day in and day out. It did not come naturally or easily, and it is the one thing I am truly proud of. Naturally I protect my skill against those who dismiss it as redundant, or old-fashioned. To get what you want—exactly the effect you have in your mind and no other—you have to have mastery, otherwise you are like a man trying to speak English with only a limited vocabulary. Unless you have that range, you end up saying what you can say, not what you mean. And once you do that you begin to tramp the road of dishonesty, persuading first others then yourself that there is no difference between the two.

❦

PERHAPS IT WAS the show that brought about such a change in you. The Show, I should call it, complete with capital letters, because it was the start of a revolution in our poor little island, was it not? When the gales of revolution, the French revolution, swept over us all, violence unleashed, the reactionaries cast aside and consigned to history, where their poor bodies now rot, a-mouldering. With you as the Robespierre, pulling strings behind the scenes, rewarding some and condemning others to professional death.

Even then, I was struck by your ruthlessness, the way you took control of the various artistic groups, rigged elections so that your creatures became the secretaries, the heads of the hanging committees, stamped out all dissent. The way you wrote manifestos and issued them in everyone's name. The way you so consistently attacked those who dared disagree with you. Dear me! The polite world of English art had not seen anything like it before; was unprepared for such an assault. Pity the poor person who got in your way. Pity Evelyn, who became an object lesson in the dangers not of opposing you but merely of not supporting you.

All this must go into my portrait, but it is difficult. In the first picture I caught it, simply because I painted what I saw but didn't understand what I was looking at. But it is all there, in the way the shadows play across the face, the way I managed to give your eyes that slightly withdrawn, waiting look. Had you asked me at the time, I would have said I was showing up your reticence, a slight fear of the world that you normally hid. I would have congratulated myself on seeing the soft core of your being. But I would have been wrong; what I was painting was your patience; the way you were waiting for the right moment before you launched out; the contempt you had for everyone—painters and critics and patrons—who needed to be disciplined, and controlled. I was painting the burning desire for power curled within you.

And in this second one, I must find a way of depicting power achieved. It would have been easier had you been a general or a politician; then I would have had five hundred years of props to make my point. I could have painted your army at its moment of triumph, and subverted the image by showing the dead and dying in their midst. Or a politician making a speech at the hustings, moulding an audience of the poor and the hungry so that they vote to remain so. Military power, political power, religious power are all well-painted phenomena; each has its attitude and stance and set of the jaw. But a critic? How to depict the power of such a man when I can follow in no giant's footsteps?

❦

YOU'RE NOT REALLY interested in how I came to live on this island, are you? At least, it would be unlike you to be so concerned. But I'll tell you anyway. It will be your punishment for that fatuous politeness you so often affect. It wasn't planned. I didn't work out in advance what was the perfect place for me. On the contrary, it took many months of wandering before I got here. Don't think, by the way, that it marks my submission to your artistic principles, that it demonstrates my acceptance of the French model. Quite the contrary. There is no art here, as you may have noticed. The fads and fancies of Paris are of no more interest to these people than they are to the aldermen of Dundee. Indeed, they think of Paris as an enemy, when they think of it at all. Spending time, energy or money on paintings is all but incomprehensible to them; fighting over it is totally so. They have the sea. It is all they have and all they need.

So I came to a place with no artistic history, where what I do is regarded with blank indifference. I am, I think, the first person ever to wield a brush on this island. There is no predecessor, no artistic colony of like-minded souls, no earnest matrons desperate to have me for tea or dinner. Just the fishermen, their stolid wives, semi-literate children and the sea.

I remember telling you once that I had always wanted to live by the sea. You, of course, thought it was about painting and went on about the possibilities for tactility in the seascape—was that the absurd word you were using then?— in the way the paint could represent light and water. You missed the point, of course. The point was to have all that nonsense washed away. Being by the sea is like a permanent baptism; the light and air hypnotises, and your soul is washed by vastness. You see what true magnificence is, and it is not something that can be put down on a canvas. When you paint, you either represent what you see or project yourself through what is in front of you. Confronted with the sea, you realise the uselessness of both. You cannot humanise the sea. It's not like all those mountains that are so popular, with merry peasants walking down tracks or harvesting corn. The sea is movement and violence and noise. You remember that Géricault painting, *The Raft of the Medusa*? A failure; a cop-out. All these people being heroic and desperate, dominating the canvas, as if they were the point. Put people on the ocean and they are irrelevant and ridiculous, not heroic. They can be swallowed up in an instant and the sea doesn't even notice. Think of that boy on the beach. But did he paint that? Did he even try to depict the magnificence of it all? No; he twisted it around so that it is yet another tale of people battling terrible odds, of human suffering and courage. How pathetic. The sea is not there for men to be heroes on.

There I go again; I know. But that is why I came here, you know; that is what I was looking for when I left England. It took some time to realise it, of course. I was making it up as I went along. When I took the train from Victoria for the Channel, I thought that I would go south, to the sun and the light, follow in the footseps of everyone else. So I did, for a while. I left my luggage at Boulogne, to be sent after me when I knew where I was going, then headed for Provence. I only stayed a few weeks; there was something in the place that disgusted my Scottish sensibilities. I could feel myself becoming sentimental, even as I stood on the balcony of a hotel in some town whose name I've forgotten. Cézanne could do it, no doubt; find the sublime in those people and landscapes. He is the only one of your protegés who is truly remarkable, head and shoulders over the rest of them. In half a dozen little pictures, he changed reality. Provence now looks like a Cézanne painting. It cannot be seen in any other way. Perhaps if I'd never gone to that exhibition of yours, I might have come up with something different, but it would not have been as good, and I was determined not to copy.

Besides, they've had it too easy. All they have to concern

them is the wind, and they complain about that incessantly.
They have never had to bellow their defiance of fate. No-one
who drinks wine grown in their own fields has. Besides,
what was I to do? Paint bull fights and olive groves? So I
moved on, headed for Spain, and stopped in a town called
Collioure; stayed there for a few weeks. But the Mediterranean! So blue, so civilised, so warm! None of the ferocity I
needed; none of the battle or the terror that the sea should
have. At least there I learnt what I was looking for, so it
wasn't a wasted voyage. It's a poor place, benighted and
grim, and I thought when I arrived that it would be perfect.
I stayed in a cheap hotel for a week, and found it very peaceful. The people have their own particular inbred beauty, but
it is a civilised place, really, if you scrape a little below the
poverty and the hardship. That "but" is important. There is a
good stone port, and castle, a handsome church, a hotel,
some shops—all too much. I got so far as negotiating to take
a little house in the village, and thought I would be happy
there. So I would have been; that was the trouble. The night
before I was due to move in, I walked along the quayside;
cloudless night, stars twinkling, a warm wind coming in off
the sea, and I felt this strange panic sweep over me. I wasn't
looking for happiness.

So on I went, waiting for that feeling of being there. Do you know what I mean? The feeling that you are home, even though you have never been there before. The sense that where you are is where you should be. I can describe it no better than that, I'm afraid. It's not a feeling you get in a big city, as when you are in London or Paris you are never anywhere in particular. So I avoided the towns and took the train slowly up through France, sometimes coming close, sometimes trying to persuade myself that I had found what I was looking for, because it was a long voyage, and a frustrating one. I wanted it over, and took no real pleasure in the trip. The landscape, the sights, the architectural marvels, were not important. They were not what I was chasing.

And I ended in Quiberon, a poor and depressing place, as I'm sure you noticed, and was not especially tempted by it. But I wandered down to the port to kill time until I could continue my journey, and saw a fishing boat unloading their catch onto the quayside. I had been looking for some time before I realised that I could understand what the men were saying. Not the understanding that is filtered through learning and education, mind, but real understanding, without even having to think. They were speaking the Gaelic. A distant variant of Scottish, of course, but close enough to the language I learned from my grandmother when I was packed off to her to live whenever my father was out of work and couldn't afford my keep. Fairly often I spent months there, and she spoke Gaelic to me only. She was a gentle woman with a fierce pride that was expressed only in these words. Unlike many, I never tried to forget the language, even though it was of little use to me.

And those fishermen reminded me of her through their conversation. A strange accent they have, with dozens of words and expressions that are different, but just recognisable. So I asked them, in Gaelic, where they came from. They found my speech as odd as I found theirs, but the curiosity of a man so obviously foreign speaking to them in something close to their own tongue tickled their fancy, and they responded. They were the first people I had had a decent conversation with in weeks, they shared a drink with me, told me of a little house which I might rent. I was home. My journey was over. I crossed over with them the next day.

I've only left a few times since, to go to the morgue in Quiberon to study my corpses or to pick up some paints and canvasses. You think I am in exile, I see myself as being in refuge. Not the first Scot to be so, either. I have an illustrious forebear. If you want, go back to the church, and look at the statue. Saint Gildas. Another man of the Clyde, although a bit before my time. I must say he had escaped my attention before I came here, but Father Charles told me all about him. Gildas fled the tumult and beastliness of England and took sanctuary on this island so he would not have to submit to the opinion of others who considered him a heretic. Thus the version of the story I was told.

A perceptive man, our priest. He says little, but sees much. You still haven't been to visit him, I note.

The islanders welcome me in their fashion, but think I'm a bit crazy as well. No-one else has chosen to live here for 1500 years, and no English—they think of me as English despite everything, which is a big disadvantage—since the smugglers were defeated half a century ago. No-one stays unless they have to, or if they can think of anywhere better to go. They don't even have any people spending the summer; nobody in their right mind would come to Houat, to this island with no running water, where it is devilish hard to get fuel for your fire or food for your plate. But here I stay, and here I would have stayed forever, had I not summoned you here and had your presence not reminded me of the advice I gave to Evelyn—that a painting unseen might as well not exist. I am thinking—no, I have decided—to go back, to re-enter the fray; but on my terms only.

What was that again? I summoned you? How dare I presume? You wrote to me, did you not, proposing the commission for a portrait? Your attempt to begin my reintroduction into the world of English art, the only one that matters to folk like us, poor though it be. To lure me back and help me take up the reins once more. No, no, my dear friend! We are trying to look below the surface now. It was I who summoned you; I who knew you would come, would have to come to see me. I lured you here. I needed to see if you would come.

I have written few letters in the past couple of years; my bank has received most of them, and they have not been so important. My demands on its services are small these days. One was important, though; the short note I wrote to your protegé Duncan a few months back. That I laboured long over, once I knew what I must do, because I knew you would read it. That was the letter which brought you here; to which you had to respond, if all was as I thought.

One sentence only, in fact, made you pack your bags and take the train to Paris, then out to Quiberon, the fishing boat over to the island, and walk across it until you arrived at my door. One short sentence made the difference. "I hope you and William are still friends; many have drowned in his displeasure."

You read things, words and pictures, with an intensity

greater than any man I have known. You seize on the little detail—a colour contrast, the shape of an ear lobe, the crook of a finger, one malformed sentence, a curious use of words, and tease it until it gives up its secrets. But what secret did my letter conceal? It tantalised, that clumsy sentence, but remained mute.

It was no slip of the pen, my friend, not a piece of babbling from someone losing touch with reality, a poor joke made by someone forgetting even the basics of English grammar. I wanted to see if you would come. It was the final test, every word considered and laboured over. Besides, I needed you here, if I was ever to break through the block which has stopped me painting anything truly satisfying.

I THINK it's time to tell you what made me leave England. You'll love it; it will appeal to your egotism. You did. It began at half past nine on a Tuesday morning, May 10, 1910. I was sitting having my breakfast, and cursing the weather, as it was dull and cloudy and I wanted brightness for a picture I was working on. At the very least I knew I would be doing nothing at least until lunchtime; maybe not even then. So I decided to read the *Morning Chronicle* and take my time over my scrambled eggs and coffee that my landlady had just brought me. I started, as I always did, with the notices and advertisements, then worked my way through the news, foreign and domestic, then, for a final pleasure, turned to the reviews.

I had been looking forward to it; Evelyn's show had opened a couple of days before, and I knew there would be something. At worst, only a little mention; at best, something more fulsome. I didn't know who'd be doing it; the *Chronicle* is always cagey about that, for some reason. It was the sort of show some young lad would be given to review, not important enough to justify paying some figure of influence. She was scarcely known, after all.

The reviews for your show had run the previous week and were dreadful, the letters from outraged colonels and academicians had followed. Your show was a perfect disaster critically, and a fine success in every other respect. In a matter of days, everybody in the country who cared for such things now knew the names of Gauguin, Seurat, Degas, and all the others.

I thought this boded well for Evelyn; she was likely to benefit from not being part of your group. Besides, I thought the critics would have exhausted their stock of vitriol on you, and would find it agreeable to say something nice for once. But no; they were having too good a time hurling abuse at the French, and most journals had passed her by to give over more space to you. Only the *Chronicle* ran a review, an anonymous one as occasionally they did. Better than nothing; any review at all was a good start. And the moment I started reading, I knew that you had written it. You have a style with words as distinct as any artist's with paint. The way you cluster adjectives, the rhythm of the sentences, the complexity of your subclauses, each one diving into another so that the meaning is almost lost as your thought races on— no-one writes like you. I'm sure I wasn't the only person who recognised it, although I could see why you didn't want your authorship generally known. You liked to think of yourself as a gentleman, after all.

We are back to my hobby horse again. The surface and the instant impression. Meet you, and one imagines you to be the perfect gentleman. Meet Evelyn for the first time, run off a sketch of her, rely on the artist's intuitive judgement and instant assessment and what do you get? A skinny little thing, who looks as though her lip might start trembling at any moment. Those slightly sloped shoulders; the sign of someone turning in on herself and afraid of reality. And sex, and femininity? Forget all that. A professional spinster, who would shudder should any man even think of touching her. A fearful timorous creature, easily broken. Inconsiderable, and not to be taken seriously. Some people stand alone because they are strong and disdain the world; others do so out of fear, desperate to belong and be accepted but not knowing how to do so, afraid of being spurned. One look and it was clear Evelyn was in the second category.

Thus the dubious insight of the modern artist. But look at her as Raphael might, that lover of women. Or Rembrandt, who saw people's souls with his godlike gaze, or Vermeer, who could paint depths and levels of calm and show the turmoil within total placidity, and you see something different again. Then you see the brittleness, the force of will which impelled her to sacrifice everything for the single goal of being a painter. Not to make a living, not to be a success; those are low things, not worth the candle. But to follow her own instincts until she was content with what she produced. She wanted my biscuit tin, to get to that point which I have approached only once in my life. But her standards were higher than mine; she was one of those souls who can never be content in this life.

You can't understand any of that; don't even pretend you can. For you art is politics, and Evelyn would not bend to your will. Why is it that you have had so much trouble with women when you find men so easy to control? Do women have to be bullied in different ways? Is another style required, one which is beyond your skill? Your wife. Evelyn. Jacky. You failed with all of them. Did they perceive something we did not? Did they see a weakness known only to yourself?

Let me look at you. Do you know, I think I must have hit on it. You are truly angry at last. Was it the slip in mentioning Jacky, perhaps? After days of provocation, you have finally opened up to me. A new emotional register on your face, which I must take into account.

Come, come! Don't be cross! I am only doing my job, you know. You have had it always too easy. No portraitist has ever pushed you this far; that's why all the pictures of you I have seen are so terrible. Oh, fine for public presentation, I have no doubt. They would look good in the dining hall of your Cambridge College, or on the walls of the Athenaeum. But they present the public face, not the inner man. They have the personality and insight of an encomium. What was it Oliver Cromwell said to Walker? "I desire that you paint me warts and all." Those other portraitists not only left out the warts, they didn't even notice they were there. Nor did I first time round. But not this time, and I am determined the next will be even better.

No; that's it for the day. I am tired, and you have been punished enough, I think. It is time we parted; I have my duties to perform.

Which ones? Oh, good heavens, there are so many of them on this island. I must make sure the tide is coming in, that the sun is setting, and that the wind continues to blow. Have you been to see the fort yet? You should; it is a sad enough spectacle to make anyone thoughtful. Built by Vauban, that great military engineer, to fend off the English. I don't believe it was ever used for that purpose. The English turned up anyway, and the good folk of this place know fine building stone when they see it. Whole walls, escarpments and abutments and whatever they call them, have vanished in the night, turned into docks and houses and shelters. One of the strongest forts in Brittany, falling to pieces because no-one loves it, while the little church, unprotected by the state and far weaker in construction, is in fine shape, sustained only by the affection of the populace. I will leave you to figure out the moral for yourself. That's where I will end up, I think. The next few days will be important, and I need to prepare myself for what is to come. I find being in that church helps me, for some reason. Father Charles encourages it; he says quiet contemplation is as good as prayer or instruction. Not that he disdains instruction, although he teaches in hints, rather than in injunctions.

I occasionally test him, which is a bit naughty of me, set

him a moral conundrum and see how he copes, all in the guise of asking for direction. What would happen, Father, if you knew of a terrible sin, but were the only person to know of it? What if you knew no-one else would believe you even if you told someone? What should you do?

"You should find a way of redeeming that sin," he replied.

Easier said than done, I replied. A fluffy answer.

"Look into yourself," he said quietly. "You are a painter. Does the sin make you angry? Then use that anger to paint. Does it make you sad? Use that. Was it a sin against another person? Try to help them. Against yourself? Then try to forgive."

But what if you can't forgive?

"Then find a way to do so. True sinners often suffer worse fates than those they hurt. Like the murderer who receives a just punishment. Then forgiveness comes more easily."

He has taught me much, the good father. I have come to rely on him greatly in the past year or so. He is a comforting presence, and has helped me more than he knows.

Come back early, if you will. There is a chill in the air first thing, and that suggests the weather is breaking up. There will be a storm soon, and that means bad light and slow progress. I need to get this all finished, otherwise the ending will be postponed for a week. You needn't concern yourself, though: it is already too late to leave. The seas are too rough, and no boat will be able to take you back to the mainland for days.

DO YOU KNOW, I had a sleepless night last night? Nothing unusual about that, I suppose, but this was worse than usual. Much worse; I tossed and turned because I was angry. Not with you particularly, but with myself. I had this sudden horrible feeling that I had made a mistake.

I should have painted you outside. Not simply because the light would have shown up your character the better, but because it would have made you uncomfortable. The inside is your sphere. The drawing room, the gallery, the dining room, the restaurant. You are a creature of the interior. Outside in the fresh air you shrivel a little, become less than yourself, a touch uncertain. Afraid, even. That fear, I realise now, is part of you, always there but hidden deep down under your never-ending movement. What are you afraid of? Not other people, or at least not anyone you have yet met. Some circumstance you know you will one day encounter but which has not yet materialised. A hint, perhaps from that long week in Hampshire when I was painting that first portrait; your son was sitting on your lap—such a good, devoted father you are—and dropped a glass on the table. It shattered and dozens of shards of glass spun across the table, onto the floor. The noise was remarkable, I remember. It didn't just break, it positively exploded. An expensive glass, too; good crystal, a present from your wife's family. Some of the fragments scudded across the table towards you. And do you know what I saw?

Let me tell you. You moved your child—both hands round his waist—you moved him very quickly a few inches as you turned your head away. But not to safety; not out of the way of the shining, twinkling fragments. Into their path. You moved your own child's body so he would serve as a shield. Oh, 'twas but a moment, but I saw it, although I forgot it immediately afterwards. It couldn't be right, could it?

Yes it could. You were prepared to use the body of a three-year-old boy to protect yourself. It was an instinctive response, a tunnel which suddenly opened up, allowing a little light to fall onto your soul. An incident of perhaps one part of a second, maybe less, before the tunnel closed once more. A laugh, a jocular remark, a good-natured reassurance that the boy was not to mind; it was only a glass. Tousled his hair. The servants called in to sweep up the mess. Another glass brought; the child sent out to play in the garden once he had been checked to make sure no sharp fragments had lodged in his clothes.

It doesn't make any difference. Or does it? Why do I feel that half a second cannot be erased by hours, days, years of different behaviour? Why is it that half a second gives the lie to a reputation for fearless courage and audacity, built up over so many years? Because it is the truth, and because the child knows it too. It is his inheritance from you, that moment. Whatever is beyond your control frightens you; that is why you must control everything and everyone. That's why I should have painted you outside. Above all here, where there is nothing but nature, and when the storms come, they are violent beyond your imagining. Not the storms of paintings, not the colourful storms of Turner, or the well-behaved and disciplined storms of someone like Vanderwelde; not something that can be neutered by three-quarters of an inch of frame. Not beautiful, either; that is a misconception. Real storms are ugly and brutal; there is little pleasing aesthetically in them; their appeal goes much deeper.

We are coming into the storm season. Shortly, perhaps even tomorrow, we will go for a walk, you and I, along the cliffs. Don't look so worried; we will wrap up well, and face your fears together, stand in the howling gale and shout our defiance at all the uncontrollable forces in the world. You must not turn me down, you will never have the opportunity again; it is a once in a lifetime offer that I am making. It will be worth it.

Shortly after I arrived here, you see, I was down at Madame Le Gurun's by the port during one of those storms. I had walked down there to see if there was any bread, but didn't realise quite how quickly the weather can deteriorate, nor how long the storms can go on. So I thought that I would have a drink and sit it out for an hour or so. It made me feel quite foolish; the storm eventually blew itself out after three and a half days. I stayed only for three hours before boredom drove me out into the worst of the rain, to walk home. How I made it I don't know, because it was pitch black and the wind was too strong for any lantern.

I got lost, and wandered too near the cliff face. Not much of a cliff, as you will see. Quite a gentle, low thing; you can scramble down to the beach in good weather, when the tide is out, and arrive scarcely even breathless. At night, in a storm, when the tide is pounding waves against the rocks, it is another matter entirely. One slip and you'd be gone; I nearly went. I was more petrified than I had ever been before in my life, and when I got home, the fire was out and a window had blown in; my papers were soaking and all over the place. A few hours of weather had reduced my life to ruins and had cut me down to a shivering, whimpering carcase. I needed a fire, urgently. And I needed to block the window. I used sketch pads for one, and a canvas I'd been working on for the other. My art saved me; the first time, to be frank, it had ever been of any use at all. I recommend both, by the way; sketch pads are good quality paper and burn well; canvas thickly covered in oil paint is a perfect way of keeping out the rain.

I ramble; my point was that while I was in the bar, a fishing boat came in, and the crew tumbled in for hot brandy to revive themselves. They were exhausted, exhilarated. The wildness of the storm had communicated itself to them. Their eyes burned, and their faces had been lashed by the rain into beauty. Even their movements had an extraordinary elegance; after fighting against the sea for many hours, moving across a room, lifting a glass, talking in a normal voice was absurdly easy. There was a life in them that burned all the more brightly because it had come close to being snuffed out altogether. And their women responded to it as well; even the most shrewish of them gathered round with renewed interest, touching them and showing in countless little ways that they were aroused by the danger. I bet that, even though some of the men were so tired they could barely stand, that many a baby was conceived that night. Storm babies, they are called.

Good life; bad art. I studied them carefully as they sat there, talking so quietly and with such animation. The high-flushed colouring of their cheeks, the animation of their eyes, their movements alternating between quickness and langour—but the langour of exhaustion, not the drawing room variety of the bored. Such ugly pictures they would have made. Those excessive colours, those poses which would be so absurd once the movement was taken out of them. You could produce a fine picture, but it would have been such a poor reflection of the reality it would scarcely be worthwhile.

How to put into paint the steam rising from their clothes, the palpable mixture of excitement and relief, the fear and the exhaustion? Not the physical tiredness; that is fairly straightforward, though still hard to do. I mean the spiritual exhaustion of someone who has faced death and been re-prieved. Someone who has to confront the fact that being alive is the thoughtless gift of the unknowing, uncaring sea. Or of God, if you prefer it, as they probably do. It cannot be done, because paintings exist only in the beholder's mind, and few people have any understanding of such violence. Such a picture would register only within the limited reper-toire of the gallery viewer. They would see the squalor of the bar, the filth of the clothes, the unshaven tiredness of the men. And would put it in the tradition of genre pictures, stretching back to the Dutch, or liken it to one of those sentimental confections of the Victorians, *The Sailors' Rest*, or some such.

And yes, I did paint it, because I was ashamed that I was still reluctant to take a chance. I worked for weeks on it, and I am proud of the result. It is the finest thing I have ever done, for I nearly fell off the cliff that night, and I had some glimpse of what true terror, and true relief, is like. I captured it in my painting.

Here it is; underneath this old pile of canvas. I won't ask you what you think; I don't care, anyway. Yes, I know; it is small, compact. Focussing entirely on two of the men, and one of the women. You see how they are huddled; the slope of their shoulders turning in on themselves? It is the colouring I am proud of most; bright blues and greens; none of the dark interior browns I would have used in the past. I have painted heroes, the equal of the Greek myths, men who have battled the gods and survived. Not the downtrodden and oppressed poor, not people you are meant to feel sorry for. You don't see it, I am sure. I can tell by your eyes. But you have never felt fear; the nearest you have come was a few fragments of glass scudding towards you across a mahogany table. You have missed something important in your life; perhaps we might rectify it before you leave. As I say, I intend to show you a storm, and there will be one before tomorrow is out.

❦

YOU MUST ADMIT I was right about the weather. Clear blue sky one day, and the next day—this; all the more impressive for being so immediate. It's cosy enough in here at the moment, mind; you will not shiver while you are with me. We will sit here in the warmth for all the world as if nothing is going on outside at all. Don't you find the noise of the wind enthralling? It sounds sometimes as though the whole house is going to be ripped off its foundations and blown out to sea. You can feel the walls shake, and the screaming of the wind outside is sometimes deafening. You wait; we're a long way from the peak yet.

But you must be chilly from the walk over, even if you are bundled up in coats and sweaters and scarves. Have you ever travelled anywhere without catering for every possible type of weather? I bet you have full morning dress back at Madame Le Gurun's, just in case. Have a glass of wine to warm you up. I've warmed it slightly by the fire, added a few extra ingredients such as you need on a day like this. Drink it down! There's plenty more, and it will make all the difference.

I am nearly done with you, you'll be glad to hear. I think this will be your last day. The finishing glazes, the last touches I can add later. I would prefer you not to be here in any case; the final manipulation of you into what I want is best done from memory, for that is the moment the picture leaves reality and approaches something altogether superior.

Yes, I have finally made up my mind. In a month or so I will pack up here and re-enter the world. It is time, and my demons are exorcised—will be, at any rate, after today.

Why today? Because today I finish. Finishing with you and going back to London are one and the same, it seems. Now I fully understand why I left in the first place. Of course, it was Evelyn who was the trigger, perhaps you have realised that already, but she was not the whole reason.

I never could figure out when exactly you decided she was an enemy. Did it start that day in the atelier? Over Sarah Bernhardt? Because she didn't want to be part of your circle of admirers? It was a long time before it took form. Let us return to that look of yours as you examined her first sketch in the atelier; that confusion I tried so hard to understand. First the look of appreciation. She was a handsome woman in her frailty; beautiful, even, in the right light; her wispiness made one want to sweep her up and protect her, or crush her.

They are the same impulse. She was tall; light brown hair done up quite primly in a way that suggested an attempt to hide deeper passions, pretending to be respectable. You appreciated that; there was some attraction.

That was part of the glance; the underlying first element. Then there was another level; the preparation of scorn. No-one you found attractive could possibly paint at all well, so you readied yourself to be patronising. A compliment. Not at all bad, my dear. Really; I have seen a lot worse. You have some talent. . . .

And then the third layer, one of confusion and shock as you looked at her sketch of that pathetic arrangement and realised that all your instincts were quite wrong. She could *draw*. In a few simple lines she had caught those objects, pinned them down and made something miraculous out of them. Yes, yes, the technique was faulty, the skill had not been learned. But there was something there you didn't expect to see, and it threw you into temporary silence. And when you did offer some comments, she scarcely heard them. She was studying what she had done and had no time for what anyone else thought.

A fault. A definite fault, so I had learned over the years. You must always listen to what other people have to say; anyone can make a useful comment, even a critic. She listened to you, but was not convinced; was not persuaded you were sole possessor of the truth. The attraction, the ability, and the deafness to your words. The three vital elements which could slowly brew up into enmity. Listen to that wind! Blowing up nicely now. More wine? Are you beginning to feel warmer? More relaxed?

I often wish I had given different advice about that exhibition at the Chenil, or that she hadn't listened to me. I wish I had told her to turn it down. Show your pictures to individuals only; wait awhile; the opportunity will come again, when you are truly ready for it. But I didn't; I said I thought she should grab the chance with both hands because that is what I would have done. But then, I did listen to other people's opinions, moulded my work to what they wanted. She took my advice, but had I not been the advocate she probably would have turned the chance down, and would not have exposed herself to you.

You do not attack merely for the pleasure of it. I must give you credit; you normally take no joy in the public demonstration of your power, as long as you have it. You could write filthy reviews of many an artist; live in London and you are spoiled for choice. But you do not. Your silence is

comment enough. Yet with Evelyn you acted out of character. What you did seemed unnecessary. The greatest critic in
the land going out of his way to pulverise an artist who is
scarcely known? Why bother?

Oh, it was effective; a little masterpiece. So many half
truths, hidden bits of violence strung together into a seam-
less quilt of polite invective. And funny! You deployed the
one thing Evelyn was truly afraid of, to be ridiculed. "It is re-
grettable that the posturings of the well-born female should
now be accorded the privilege of public exhibition, when
once they surfaced only when the men had been left to their
brandy." "There may be a few who find genius in mediocrity; this reviewer, alas, is immune to its charms. . . ." "There
are failures that are complete, and failures that are partial,
tho' if anyone paints enough, consistency in poorness cannot be assured." You see, I can recall every word.

And then the demolition of the pictures; every bit as thor-
ough as the job you did on poor Anderson. Except that you
tried too hard; you overstretched yourself, and strove for effect.
No metaphor left undoubled, no sentence simply put. When
you took Anderson to pieces your language was spare; this was
florid. With him you were direct and spoke in words un-
adorned; with Evelyn no literary device—and you are master

of them all—was unused. But it was empty, your abuse. No reason was given for your opinions, no arguments were advanced. You did not prove her inadequacy, merely asserted it.

For the first time in all the years I had known you, you had lied. You stepped over an invisible but crucial line. I had long had my doubts about the importance you gave yourself, but I could never before claim that you were anything other than an honest man. With that article you entered the darkness of calumny and deceit. The last threads of loyalty snapped, completely and irrevocably. You lost your protection, the only thing which gave immunity from vengeance. The only thing which had always made me forgive you.

Because her paintings were good. You knew they were good, and you had known it ever since you first met her. You unleashed your power in an ignoble cause, to protect and advance yourself alone. You became an outlaw, acknowledging no restraint but your own power. You sinned against the very art you existed to protect and nourish. And you know what I think about sin. And punishment, of course. Let me fill your glass once more. I see the colour coming back into your face nicely now.

It wasn't even about her pictures, was it? Nor even your desire that there should be no challenges to those Frenchmen you were championing. Nor even her dismissive attitude to you. Had it not been a review of her exhibition, you would have found something else. Some humiliation, some slight, the more public the better. Because you were frightened, desperate. You thought the triumph that you had just won might be torn from your grasp, that your reputation might be ruined.

Shall I tell you how I am so sure? Because you are here. Because I wrote Duncan a letter with that phrase in it—"many have drowned in his displeasure"—and you came, after nearly four years of forgetting that I existed.

I was surprised by the whole business, I must admit. Trumpeting the bohemian ethic in a literary journal is one thing, taking part in it yourself is quite another. I always assumed yours was a paper amorality, designed to titillate the salons but not so much that it reduced your standing. Even so, many a man has survived worse scandal with their reputation enhanced. Or was it an aesthetic matter? Was it, perhaps, that you didn't mind the world knowing you had accidentally sired a little reproduction of yourself, but recoiled at the idea of who the mother was? Did you shudder at the idea of the sniggers that might go around if it became known that you were conducting a squalid little bedsit affair with a woman of such epic vulgarity?

With Jacky, of all people? A man such as yourself should

bed only the crème de la crème, no? The greatest poetesses, the daughters of earls, playwrights or artists. Or at least someone with five hundred a year of her own. Not the artistic equivalent of a flower girl. Such people are all very well for artists. Expected, even. But for a critic? Dear me, no! And to commit the solecism of getting the woman pregnant? Oh, the fun of it!

So unlikely that my incredulous laughter was instrumental in persuading your wife that her unease was merest fantasy. You owe me much. The first I heard of any of it came from her, and she was so bothered at her suspicions and jealousy she came to me specifically, and risked humiliation to raise the subject. She wrote, asking to see me over a matter of some importance. I was bemused and agreed, not least because I wished to find out what it was all about. She had always rather disapproved of me; I was not her sort of person at all. She had not forgotten my visit to Hampshire to paint your portrait, and did not forgive bad behaviour. The very idea that she might need me I found somewhat exciting.

She arrived exactly on time—she was as punctual as you were late. Curiously, I had little experience with dealing with lady visitors; the only women who ever came to my studio were either models or clients. I did not know what to do with her, and all the inadequacies of my upbringing burst forth. I felt as though I should offer her tea or something, and the realisation that even after all these years I could still be made uncomfortable by a woman like her brought out all my natural rudeness.

I think she very nearly left without explaining why she'd come, but she was desperate. Eventually my discomfort exhausted itself and I asked her what she wanted, although I imagine I added something to the effect that if she could be quick then I would be able to get back to my work. No-one could say I wheedled my way into her confidence; quite the contrary.

"It is about William," she began. "Have you heard any stories about him?"

"Many," I replied. "He is one of those people who generates stories; it is part of the way he has become influential."

Her distress was by now so obvious even I could not bring myself to continue her torment. She was beginning to look absurd, and that was unfair for someone so naturally sure of herself. Quite old-fashioned, she is; I had never realised it before. Something of a survival of the last century, tightly bound into her clothes, straight-backed and unbending. No-one would want to paint her now, I think; she does not have a modern air. Millais, perhaps, might have done her justice, and conveyed that plush velvet and window-closed soul of hers. I felt myself beginning to lose interest, so told her to sit down and explain a little more clearly what she wanted. It was not what I said, you understand, but the way that I said it that made all the difference. She only needed the barest hint of sympathy to let loose all her woes and become a different person entirely.

"I have been worried for the last few months. You no doubt think me a silly woman, with foolish ideas. But William has always been the best of husbands. . . ."

"Indeed he has. I have often wondered how he manages it. I know I never could. But then, he is married to you, and that is a powerful incentive to good behaviour."

She blushed. "I know that men are not like women," she began, "and I know that being faithful does not come easily to them. . . ."

"Oh. I see." Her look of steely self-control as she brought herself to this point was far better explanation than anything she had said.

"Have you noticed anything, or heard anything? I know you would not think it proper to say, but if you knew the agonies I have suffered in the last few months, you would pity me."

I had a choice here, you see. My response could take two

forms; I could exploit the situation, feed her fears, offer her false sympathy and reap the rewards. For they were on offer, you know. That most virtuous of women could easily have fallen into my arms then with only the slightest encouragement. Millais's women were often fallen, or about to fall. What a glorious triumph it would have been! And rather a pleasurable one, I imagine. I was always intrigued by that combination of icy control and the occasional flash of the eye, the way the façade sometimes failed to hide a hint of hunger. But, alas, you were my friend.

I sprang to your defence. I had seen nothing and heard less. Which was true, I had seen progressively less of you over the years; we were moving ever more definitely in different circles. Had you been having a grand affair, no doubt I would have noticed. But Jacky was not the sort of person you took to the opera, or entertained to lavish dinners. A squalid little encounter once a week in a Bermondsey boarding house could easily pass unnoticed, although when we were closer I would have caught even that. Only a wife might notice something amiss, and then not enough to form any solid conclusions. So I told her that any changes she noticed should be put down to your preoccupation with this great exhibition you were planning. She had to understand how all-consuming such a thing could be. "It is a terrible thing to say of a man, but faced with a choice between Cleopatra and a painting of Cleopatra, William would take the canvas." She should not worry, I told her, firmly but gently. All would be well and her foolish fears would be soon forgotten.

She left soon after, giving me a look of such gratitude I half regretted my altruism. I bathed in the warm glow of my virtue for some time afterwards. But as she stood by the door, she turned, and her face hardened. "I am glad of what you said. It is the one thing I would never have forgiven in him." And, by God, she meant it. The calm way she said it frightened even me, and I had nothing to do with it. I never realised quite how proud, quite how conventional she was. You must have known all too well, and knew what her reaction was likely to be. How would it be, William, to have to earn your own living for once? To give up the house, the works of art, the weekends at country houses, the balls? To have to become one of those hand-to-mouth bohemians you praise at a distance? That's what her look implied. Having a mistress might be acceptable in Chelsea; it was not in Mayfair, and certainly not with a wife like yours. You tried to straddle both worlds, and for the first time you risked losing your balance.

So how could you make such a slip? I do not ask how you could do such a thing, consort with a common shop girl when a beautiful if somewhat well-controlled woman was already yours. That is all too clear; there is something quite horrible in a woman who will not bend to your will, when everyone else not only bends but breaks at your very nod. But the magnitude of the mistake! You, who had never taken a false step in your life! That is something I cannot understand. It almost makes you human. Almost makes you deserve sympathy—would do, except for the way you reacted. But Jacky? What was it? Was it sleeping with a woman artists slept with? Is that your frailty, that all along that was what you wanted to be? Does your unstoppable desire to control and direct painters come from a frustration at not being one yourself? I cannot believe it, and yet I cannot think of any other reason why you would choose her. Did you talk of tactility with her, after the passion had passed? Seek her opinion on Post-Impressionism? Or did you enter into her enthusiasms and quiver with anticipation as she showed you her latest rouge? Or was it the squalor of it that you needed; some respite from the beauty and aestheticism? A sordid and furtive animality to act as counterpoint to all that refinement. I hope you were satisfied with your choice, but I doubt it. You were no more able to arouse Jacky than I could, of that I am sure. Perhaps it was the payment that excited you, the reduction of human emotion to cash transaction?

I am being provocative; I apologise; I do not wish to set your weak heart a-flutter. There is a reason for it, though. I would like to see you angry again, to see you lose control for once in your life, in my presence. Otherwise Jacky will have triumphed over me, for you lost control with her, did you not? Hence the grey-green in my picture, to set off the shadows and echo the darkness back into your face. You will see it soon enough. The shadow in the background, the perfect man with the monumental flaw. The way the light falls on your face and is absorbed, so that there is a hint of something hidden behind. It is the fear that is in your life; a contrast with the earlier portrait, which has none of that, which has the blue and red of boundless self-confidence, of a world waiting to be tamed, a man who does not know his own weakness. Combine that with a slight hunching of the shoulders, as if you are protecting your soul from reality, and the point will be made, for those who can see. Only a true friend can do that, put that in. Only me.

I know about it only because Jacky came to see me a few weeks before her death to ask my advice, because I was your friend and would know best what to do. And because she feared to say anything to Evelyn, her friend and confidante, who could have given your wife a lesson or two in puritanism, so I thought. She shook her head when I suggested Evelyn might be a more appropriate person to talk to. "I couldn't," she said. "She'd never talk to me again." There was fear in her as she said that; she made me promise I would tell no-one; certainly not Evelyn. Only I was to know.

Which just shows how desperate the poor girl was. Do you know what she said? That she had "compromised herself with a gentleman." I was so delighted with the phrase— if you try it you will find it rolls around the mouth like a fine cigar—that I didn't quite grasp what she was talking about for a while. She wanted to know what to do. She arrived at my studio just as I was beginning work, so I was probably rather brusque with her; I thought she probably wanted money or something to get her jewellery back from the pawnbrokers.

But no; she was compromised. And with a gentleman. I suppose a working man would merely have got her into trouble. Her face was a picture. I don't mean that harshly, you understand. I'm not being comical. But as a model she always had this perfect deadpan look about her. No frown or smile ever troubled that pink face of hers; not with me, in any case. I didn't hire her for her emotional register. Now, all of a sudden, she was a portraitist's dream. The levels of emotion were extraordinary; shame, despair, hope, the pleasure of attention, fear. And something else as well, which I couldn't pin down. Something fierce, almost animal-like. It was that look which ultimately brought you to sit in my chair here.

The interaction was ludicrous, of course; she talked in this bizarre language which was her own special parody of a drawing room conversation, so it was difficult to understand her at times. But eventually all became clear enough. She was pregnant; you were the father; and what could she do about it.

My initial reaction was one of complete indifference, once the astonishment at your foolishness had subsided. Such things happen, and they happen to people like her all the time. But then there was that fierceness. Do you know, I do believe things might have turned out differently had her expression not been so magnificent, and if she had not placed herself—quite by chance—by the window so the early morning light illuminated it perfectly? The way that emotion transformed her from a silly little woman into a queen, an empress, a goddess, even; the way her eyes shone and her skin took on a fiery grandeur; the tilt of her head as pride and defiance took over her soul. I could have sat her down and painted her then and there, just for that look. I knew that I should do my best to banish it, make sure that it never crossed her face again, to put out that light in her eyes forever. But it would have been a sin to do so. She was beyond beautiful, and her beauty was caused by the thought of that child. So I didn't try to persuade her to do the sensible thing and go to the angel-maker, as the French so delicately say. Not because of her, or you, or because of what was right, but because of the effect of the light turning on her face. I gave her what she truly wanted. She hoped I would lend her the money for the abortionist. I told her to have the baby.

And, I may say, I gave her some practical advice as well. That she should write you a letter informing you of what had happened, and asking you to contribute to the upkeep of your joint creation. I considered for a moment that she should also assure you that the secret would be safe in her hands. That she would not approach you nor threaten you in any way. That she would leave London and be as discreet as if she did not exist. But I decided against the idea. No, I thought. Let him sweat a bit. Let's worry him a little. It'll make him more generous. A mistake. I underestimated you.

Good God, man! All she wanted was ten shillings a week! Less than you spend on wine. She had nothing, and wanted nothing except that little brat. And she knew what she was giving up, as well. She knew that her chances of a dutiful husband and a little parlour and a respectable life would all but vanish once she had someone's bastard on her hands. Even her friendship with Evelyn might well evaporate. She would be all on her own, and she was willing to take the risk. It wasn't much she was asking of you, and it wasn't blackmail. Even had you refused, she wouldn't have done anything. She wasn't like you.

But that was not the point, was it? The point was that she decided to defy you, go against your wishes. And that was unforgiveable. And even more unforgiveable were the actions of the person behind this plot to blacken your reputation. Jacky could never have written that letter to you; it was too well-phrased, too suggestive. Too well spelt. So who could it be? Who in your circle could be behind this? Not Henry MacAlpine, for example, who would never dare attack you, who was too much the fawner and flatterer. No; only one possible person who knew Jacky could give her such advice. Your attention turned to Evelyn.

What did you see in your mind—the two women, sitting together, giggling as they plotted to destroy your marriage, bring you to ruin? The ruthless fury of womanhood scorned, relentless in their pursuit, never resting until they had taken their revenge? Did you imagine that she was going to start spreading stories about you? That she would write to your wife? Did you think that Evelyn wanted a hold over you, to guarantee that you favoured her? Were you so puffed up with your own importance and so sure that everyone had the same values as you did?

They paid a heavy price, by God they did. When I read about Jacky being dragged out of the river, my heart skipped a beat. The reporter quoted the police. Part-time prostitute, pregnant, killed herself in desperation. Happens all the time. Open and shut, no mystery, racing results from Sandown in the next column. Maybe it was even true. How should I know? I have no evidence to suggest otherwise, except for the memory of the way her face glowed in the light through my window. A woman like that wants to live, will do anything to cling on to life. Such a person needs the life torn from her by force.

Did she scream and struggle, William? Did her fingernails scratch on the stone parapet? Did she thrash in the water before she went under? Did she hear you as you crept up behind her in the dark? Probably not, because even Jacky could have taken you on in a fair fight. And what about you? Was your poor weak heart thudding, threatening to tear itself from its moorings as you pushed her? Did you hurry away with your cloak up around your face? Or did you stay and keep watch, to make sure she sank and never came to the surface again? I don't even ask if you felt remorse, or guilt. I know you too well; you decided it was necessary. It was done. She was punished for her impudence. She didn't matter. People don't, do they?

One more glass of wine; but no more. I don't want you falling asleep on me, you know, and it is easy to do if you have too much of this. It is a deceptive brew, more potent than it seems when you drink it.

You cannot send a man to the gallows because of a tilt of the head in the sunlight. Not when you are so desperately trying to convince yourself that it cannot be true, when you range over your memories, reorganising your past to persuade yourself that a friend could not possibly do such a thing. Suppose I went to the police. They would make enquiries, and conclude there was no substance to the suggestion. But you would hear of it, and know who had said such a thing. So I kept quiet once more, and a week later you moved on to ensure that nothing Evelyn ever said about you, nothing she knew or suspected, would have any effect either.

I saw Evelyn after Jacky was found, and she had seemed calm enough on the surface, at least. Those years of careful upbringing were being put to use. She was most upset, she said, in an even voice. Upset, distressed, but not overly so.

She passed no comment on the circumstances but politely, and somewhat coldly, took her leave. Her exhibition was to open the following day, she had a lot still to prepare. She was anxious.

Why should she be any more than regretful, after all? Jacky was just a model, however valued. A friend, perhaps, but what friendship can there really be between two such people, so different in outlook, upbringing, temperament and tastes? And many people become preoccupied, distracted, when they are preparing for a show. I put it out of my mind, in the same way that I tried not to think of Jacky. I succeeded there; I even forgot to go to the funeral. I was working, trying something new and different which I couldn't get right. I kept trying and trying, almost stopping but then going back for one last attempt. And when I finally gave up, the effect I was chasing still unachieved—it was too late.

I knew I should feel guilty about my callousness, so when I saw the review of Evelyn's exhibition, I thought I would expiate my sin by going round and making sure she was all right. Better to succour the living than waste time on the dead, who hardly need our support anymore. So I went round to her studio, though I didn't know if she had even seen the review, or worked out who had written it. She was the sort who didn't bother reading a paper, after all, and many a painter studiously avoids them until their exhibition is long closed. I guessed, of course, that she'd be upset if she had. Who would not be? It is a horrible thing to be publicly brutalised like that. You do not know, of course; you have only carried out such assaults, never yet been on the receiving end. The way the mind reacts is interesting, I suppose; an incredulity followed by a rising desire to turn away, which is so easily defeated by the necessity of reading it all. The battle to remain detached, unconcerned, the slow realisation that this defence is crumbling. The mounting panic as the words flow over you, metaphor by metaphor, insult by insult. The terrible fear that what you are reading is the truth, not merely the opinion of one biased, malevolent man. The way the words come as you answer the charges—words which no-one will ever hear, for you know there can never be any response; the critic will never have to account for himself. It is not done.

And then, the hatred. The blind but utterly impotent loathing of the man who has done this, so coldly. The way obtuseness has become insight, and stupidity intelligence, and cruelty a passing entertainment for the reader. The realisation that the review was written with pleasure, seeing in your mind's eye the smug look of self-satisfaction as it is finished.

Finally, the belief, as all your defences and self-confidence suddenly crumble. The belief that the words are true, that you have been exposed for what you are, because the words are there, in print, on the page. The overwhelming conviction that what you are reading has an authority which overwhelms your self-belief, that the author has seen through you and exposed you for the fraud you really are. And this lasts, believe me. It does not go away quickly or easily, however strong you are. They gnaw at you, those words, bring you to the brink of madness, because you cannot shake them out of your mind. Everywhere you go you hear them, echoing in your mind. Only the most worldly, most cynical, can resist their power. You could, no doubt. I couldn't, which is why I toadied to people like you for so long, and had to come here when I decided to do so no longer.

Ah! My friend, it is another—yet another—experience you have missed in your life, that realisation that someone wishes to do you harm, and has successfully done so without meeting any resistance. It is a great hole in your existence.

So I realised she might well be distressed; but I supposed that fury would sustain her, especially if she realised who was the author. She had, as you always guessed, a very high opinion of herself. It is odd how the greatest arrogance can be contained within the most timid creatures. Besides, she didn't like you, although she was too polite ever to say so.

Her opinion was contained in a vague shadow that once passed over her eyes when you were mentioned.

It took me about an hour to get to Clapham, I remember, and I also remember becoming annoyed as I walked, because it was drizzling with rain and cold; annoyed with you for what you had done, annoyed with Evelyn's possible unhappiness, and annoyed with myself, because I discovered that I could not even rush to the side of a beloved colleague and friend without thinking of myself. Not only seeing myself offering aid and comfort, but also feeling irritated because my working day had been disrupted. That was callous of me, was it not? Truth is everything, and I cannot pretend to gallantry I did not feel. I was preoccupied with a picture I was trying to complete for the New English exhibition; my portrait of that Woolf woman, and I was proud of it. It was a good likeness, which captured her odd mixture of discontent and complacency, and she had already made it clear that she disliked it. She never said so, of course—that would have spoiled her notion of herself as being above such vanities— but I was getting under her skin, tormenting her a little by showing her things she could never see in a mirror.

But it wasn't there yet, and I had worried about it all week and almost decided to give Evelyn a miss for a day, so I could worry some more. Eventually my notion of chivalry triumphed, and I did not turn back on Westminster Bridge and retrace my steps to my easel. I never did finish that painting, in fact, and it was one of the ones I threw out when I left. But I left my mind back in the studio, along with my brushes, and thought about my composition all the time as I walked to Clapham, thought about it as I rang the doorbell and exchanged pleasantries with the landlady, and still thought about it as I tiptoed up the stairs and opened the door.

And still thought about it as I stood there, in the doorway, looking at Evelyn's body, hanging there from the big iron hook in the centre of the room. I was annoyed; only later did I try to construct a feeling of anguish, but that didn't cover it up at all. A woman, one I loved, was dead, and I was annoyed that I might not now get a portrait finished in time. It's these moments, I think, that reveal the true man; the instinctive reaction before manufactured and trained good behaviour can take over. You have a glimpse of what lies underneath the conventional responses, and in my case I saw a monumental selfishness.

Well, shock, perhaps. The mind sometimes cannot absorb certain things and takes refuge in the normality of daily concerns. I still think that is merely an excuse. I do not know how long my initial annoyance would have lasted, how long I would have stood in the doorway staring, how long it would have been before I came back to life and did something. Not that there was anything to do. She was dead, had been for hours. Methodical as ever, she'd prepared it all with care. Thick cord, obviously newly bought from a shop, just the right length. Proper slip knot, stand on a chair, and—kick. No chance of changing her mind at the last moment, no way of getting out of it. She wanted to die and she did. She was competent at everything she attempted.

And I saw the result. The face contorted and discoloured, the tongue sticking out, the odd angle of the neck, the looseness of the limbs. The chandelier pushed out of true by her body hanging at an angle, its cheap glass decorations tinkling slightly as the wind came through the door. A still life, all femininity eradicated and, like the boy on the beach, the image has stayed with me ever since.

A carefully arranged tableau. On the desk was the newspaper, open at the page with your review, and at the bottom she had written in a small, neat hand, "written by William Nasmyth." She knew, you see. Does it comfort you, William, that even a woman in such distress could recognise your style? That your personality is so distinctive it proclaims itself even in such circumstances? I hope it makes you swell with pride; it is quite an achievement, after all.

But you had a still greater triumph, for beside the newspaper with your review was another, with the notice of Jacky's death inside it. And underneath that, the same hand had written, "ruined by Henry MacAlpine."

She thought I was the father of that child, William! She thought I had driven Jacky to her death, that I had shamed one and betrayed the other, taken her friend away from her. She held me responsible for it all, and never knew about you! Doesn't that make you laugh, at last? You must see the funny side, surely, the thought of that woman hanging there, dying by her own hand, cursing me with her last breath! I didn't take it in; I didn't want to take it in, and so I allowed myself to be distracted. I turned away from her body, and saw the last part of her careful *mise en scène*.

Around the walls, turned to face the room for the first time, were all those paintings she hadn't put into her show, which she had been so frightened of me seeing.

Pictures of Jacky, painted in a way I could never have managed, and which made me realise all my failings. She had painted a person, not merely a model striking a pose to challenge the artist's skill. Her Jacky had character, personality. She was a real woman, suffused with emotions, tenderly and gently depicted, not some mannequin hiding behind the blank face of compliant stupidity. She had seen through the coarseness, the silliness, and found something beautiful; not merely a voluptuous body which I saw while I spent my time showing what a clever technician I was. Jacky sitting, lying on the sofa, curled up in front of the fire; in each one she saw something special and touching, and painted it with a loving hand. And her self-portraits shone with warmth as she sat close to Jacky and looked into her eyes, or with loneliness when the room was empty. This was what she had wanted, what no man could provide, why she rejected me out of hand. I could never have brought out those expressions in her; didn't know it was possible.

But there were others as well, pictures of both of them entwined, stretched out together, passionate and unrestrained, intimate and pornographic, doing things that even now make me shudder. Shocking pictures, with faces distorted by depravity, bodies twisted out of shape in their striving for each other. And she had used the light, not hidden herself away in darkness. By God, she had used it as no one had ever tried before. Each picture was suffused with brilliant dazzling colours, the flesh tones green and purple and red, the sun shining off sensuous limbs that splayed out in ways no life model could ever emulate. The complex bundle of angles and curves on their bodies. Celebrating even as they abused the majesty of the human form, God's image, and reduced it to the obscene and the grotesque. The sun shining through the windows even gave them haloes as they mauled each other, as though their depravity was the stuff of saints. The eyes, too, I remember, staring out so calmly, shining brightly as they gazed out of the frames, daring me to disapprove, amused at my shock. No gallery could ever put such things on its walls. No man could ever have painted them. I never imagined a woman would ever dare.

Even now those pictures haunt me; I dream of them, they come to me unbidden as I lie in bed at night; I try to put them out of my mind but even now, after four years, I cannot. I've tried everything—long walks, sleeping draughts of every sort prepared by the pharmacists of Quiberon, prayer, confession. Nothing works. These were not subtle paintings; not Manet's *Olympia,* where all is left to the imagination, the pose so careful and decorous, the viewer drawn into the picture so that the obscenity is in your mind and the painter can plead innocence. There was no coyness about these. Anyone who looked at them was an intruder who had no right to be there. I remember one most of all; Jacky was on her knees in front of Evelyn who was naked on the sofa. There was no joy on her face: this was not a portrait of the lover touched by the divine. This was devilish and violent, her face twisted, her body tense, an exultant scream coming from her mouth. What could that have to do with love or tenderness? This could not be that frail, dainty woman I knew? But like your moment with the shattered glass, I knew this was the truth. This was what she truly was, degraded and foul.

Those pictures made me tremble; I thought it was the shock of seeing Evelyn hanging there, but it wasn't. It was knowing her for the first time, and being revolted by the way she let loose what was within her and revelled in it. To do such things, think such thoughts and paint it as love. Not to see it for what it was, what it must be, but to turn it into art such as no-one has attempted before.

It was the scream of her landlady, coming up the stairs to bring her a pint of milk, stopping behind me as she saw inside the room, dropping the bottle on the floor so it smashed and the milk ran into the room, that brought me back to reality. Or rather knocked me out of it entirely, for I scarcely remember a single thing after that. Not of what happened, in any case. I suppose someone called the police, the doctors, somebody must have cut her down, taken her off to the morgue. Presumably some member of her family arrived, at some stage. I must have given statements to the police, talked to her father. I do not remember any of it. All I know is that eventually I was on a cross-channel ferry, feeling I could breath again for the first time in weeks. Between opening the door to her room and hearing the hooter of the ferry leaving the harbour, there was nothing at all except the memory of those pictures.

As the days and weeks passed I became ever more angry at her for daring to have a life unseen and unsuspected until you destroyed the only two things she truly valued and brought it all into the light. You cast down a terrible, perverted animal; even the wildest of bohemian London would have recoiled at those images, been overwhelmed and revolted by their passion and power. The work that was truly close to her heart, which came from what she was, could never be shown in public to anyone. Should I have been grateful to you, William? You exposed Evelyn for what she truly was, made me see the error of my ways in even being friends with her. Should I not thank you, old friend, for rendering yet another service to me?

But you destroyed much of me, as well. You took away my belief that I could see people in their faces and know them. You took away someone I loved and replaced her with something monstrous and twisted. The Evelyn I knew I can now scarcely recall; all there is left is that picture leaning against the wall, and the corpse which swung there, hating me as she died. Had your ruthlessness not intervened, nothing would have changed; I would never have known. Life could have gone on, and I would have my wife and house in Holland Park, my students and my riches.

For much of my exile I have hated her, but of late that has become weaker; even that terrible picture can no longer excite my disgust in the way it once did. I wish you had seen it; she *was* a good painter, you know, something extraordinary, and this was proof that would have convinced even you. She had taught herself to experience the extremes of passion and had learnt how to turn it all into painting. No-one I know has ever come close. Can I hate forever someone who managed such a thing? Who succeeded when I always turned away and flinched, compromised and sought the good opinion of people like yourself instead? Who was prepared to risk all and lose everything? Of course I hate her for where it all came from. I have abused her and scorned her memory for being what she was. I have tried to learn how to wish her soul happiness, and to mean it. But I cannot; not even the church can accomplish such miracles, it seems. My forgiveness lies only in the memory of her achievement, awful though it was.

I will cast her out entirely, now; she must not find any further place in my thoughts. I will find another way of calming my nights, so I no longer see those images when I close my eyes. I will forget them, and then they will have gone forever. I will replace them with the image of another friend, more twisted than she was. I have painted your soul in this picture, William, as much as I can; you may look at it now. Come; I will turn it round so you can see it without having to move; I think that wine I gave you is responsible for making it so difficult for you to stand. The strong flavour you so dislike hides many things. Don't worry; it will do no more than make you a little groggy. I know this; my sleepless nights have made me experiment with many a potion, and I know the effects of them all. This particular one merely induces a certain lassitude and weakness, but does not bring any sort of oblivion.

Now, what do you think? You can look at yourself as you are. Do you see the coldness I have put in around your eyes? The cruelty of the mouth, the calculation of the chin? I hope you notice that the background is entirely dark, for there has never been anyone in the world but yourself. The shadows I am particularly proud of, there is no dominant light source, you see; rather it seems as though the light comes from within you. You illuminate the canvas, because you are the source of all certainty and truth. Set it up beside the older one and you will see the point I'm making, I hope. All the cleverness, the intelligence, is still there, the cultivation and the appreciation of beauty. But you have wasted your gifts, used them wrongly, lost the right to possess them.

Do you know, I'm proud of this? It really is a very good

likeness of you. Deceptively easy on the eye, at first glance; only if you look closely do you begin to see its subtleties. I've come a long way in the past few years, I think. I am beginning to paint what I want to paint, rather than an approximation of it.

It's not finished, of course. You can see that, certainly. You miss nothing where painting is concerned. It's unbalanced. The first is a portrait of a man whole in mind and body; the second shows the corruption of the soul, but as you have noted, I have been a little flattering over your appearance. I've made you a touch younger-looking, less weakened than you are. A deliberate trick on my part; I am not falling back on old habits. The parallel corruption of the body will come in the last part of the triptych, which I will begin soon. It will never be seen while I am alive, of course; never could be, any more than Evelyn's could be shown. But she taught me that is no reason for not painting something; perhaps the most truthful pictures must be hidden.

I don't know, and I don't really care. All I know is that I am looking forward to the challenge of the next part of this project. It will not escape me this time; it will be no rapid sketch for a newspaper, no missed opportunity or failure. I will work on you until I have you down, have no fear of that.

I told you, I think, how I could not get that boy, because I did not know him in life. He was abstracted, just a pattern of shapes and colours. I will rectify that. I will heighten those greens without fear; make the eyes confront the viewer more directly. The way the sea erodes the flesh and exposes the bone structure I will depict with love. It will be an extraordinary work, something that will stick in the memory and replace those images that dance in my head when I try to sleep. A work that will last for all time. Worth the effort, I think. Even you would approve, critic though you are. I can see it in my mind so clearly.

I hope you understand all this; it is at your bidding, really. You are the one who suggested I go back to England, after all, and this is the only way I can think of which will allow me to return with an easy conscience. I couldn't spend the rest of my life watching your success and knowing that at your heart you are a cruel, pitiless man, who can destroy others without a second thought. Surely you realise that? Such a person deserves no admiration or happiness. I could not accept a good review from you, nor yet a bad one. I could not belong to any club, show in any exhibition, be associated with any gallery, which had contact with you, and you have contacts with them all. I could not tolerate your sin and your success. I toned in your skin with green and brown in my portrait, shadowed your face to show that I understood the darkness of your mind.

This one on the easel here can go to the Royal Academy exhibition; it will make a fine last tribute to an old friend and will probably rekindle my career very handsomely. They won't realise the flattery they see is more than mere obsequiousness, and will pay to have the same in their own portrait; I will happily oblige them. Then I'll present this one to your widow; I was the last person to see you alive, your oldest friend; it will be a kind gesture to assuage her grief. She will be grateful and—who knows?—maybe more than gratitude will result. I would make her a better husband than you did, old friend.

❧

THE STORM is reaching its peak. We must hurry; sometimes they blow out so qui ckly you are almost deafened by the sudden silence as the wind drops from gale force to nothing in a matter of seconds. You must experience its power at first hand, otherwise you will never understand what I have been talking about. It will make the days you have spent sitting listening to me worthwhile. You must try, even though you are so feeble now; I will support you and ensure you get there. Do not worry. I will guide you to the best vantage point, so you can see what violence really is.

We will take the path by the cliffs, I think. It is beautiful on a night like this, with the wind blowing and the ground still wet and slippery from the rain. All alone, for no islanders will be out on a night like this. You will feel that surge of danger I have mentioned, and know what it is to be afraid. It is more exhilarating than you can imagine, for it is foolhardy to venture near the edge. Many a man has slipped along there, and there is always the risk of falling into the sea. No-one could save anyone who does, no matter how quickly they run to the village and raise the alarm. Not even a strong swimmer could survive the undercurrents and avoid being dashed to pieces on the rocks, to be washed up, torn and broken, when the sea is finished with him.

Come with me now. I will not take no for an answer.

With thanks to Felicity Bryan, Julie Grau, Lyndal Roper,
Nick Stargardt, and more than ever, Ruth Harris.

Iain Pears was born in 1955. Educated at Wadham College, Oxford, he has worked as a journalist, an art historian, and a television consultant in England, France, Italy, and the United States. He is the author of seven highly praised detective novels, a book of art history, and countless articles on artistic, financial, and historical subjects, as well as the international bestseller *An Instance of the Fingerpost*. He lives in Oxford, England.